THE REJECTED WRITERS' CHRISTMAS WEDDING

A SOUTHLEA BAY NOVEL

SUZANNE KELMAN

Text copyright © 2018 by Suzanne Kelman

Published by Goody2 Publishing, Seattle

www.suzannekelmanauthor.com

ISBN-13:

ISBN-10:

Cover design by Blondie's Custom Book Covers

Printed in the United States of America

Dedicated to my very own bridegroom, Matthew Wilson. Thank you for twenty-six amazing years of the perfectly crafted "happily ever after" story to inspire a storyteller for life.

Always and forever.

CHAPTER ONE

RABID ALIENS AND ELVES ON FIRE

It wasn't unusual to see people running in our picturesque Northwest town. In fact, it was quite a commonplace occurrence, especially in the summer, when the lovely view of the Cascade Mountains and the cool shore breezes afforded a very pleasant running experience. But no sane person ran in November, when it was below freezing, at a pace akin to someone on fire, especially somebody dressed as a Christmas elf.

So when I urged the members of the Rejected Writers' Book Club to look out the large Southlea Bay Library window at the sprinting postmistress, none of us could believe our eyes.

"Maybe she lost a sack of Santa's letters," I quipped from my view at the library check-in desk, where I worked daily, having been distracted moments before by the crash of flailing doors ricocheting ungraciously off the red brick walls of the post office building.

Upon my report of this small-town phenomenon, a few choice members of the Rejected Writers' Book Club, who had gathered for a reading of *Jane Eyre*, scattered copies of Miss Brontë's book about willy-nilly, like a bunch of toddlers emptying out a box of Legos, then, in one unanimous move, bounded to the window for a better view. They now congregated to stare, their mouths agape.

I, too, couldn't help but watch with amusement as I followed the little soccer ball–shaped woman as she, adorned with customary elf bells, jingled and jangled her way down Main Street, one hand placed firmly across her ample bosom.

As we all continued to track her journey, there was much discussion about whether anyone could ever recall seeing Mrs. Barber run before. This was followed by each member laying bets on where she was going.

But much to Lavinia's chagrin, she did not stop at the Crab Apple Diner, Southlea Bay's favorite family restaurant; nor did she head to the French-style florist, All Stems from Here, with its cheery pink-and-white-striped awnings, which Ruby had been so certain about. Or even Happy Paws Animal Clinic, which Annie would have put money on. As Mrs. Barber blew by Ruby-Skye's Wool Emporium, all bets were off, and the assemblage shuttled to the next window for continuous coverage.

Like a herd of sheep at feeding time, they trotted behind each other as they navigated their way from window to window, winding their way around the fiction section, then history, until they ended up all the way back behind handicrafts. But as Mrs. Barber continued to sprint, the onlookers ended up stacked like a pile of kittens, peering out through their last hope: a narrow letterbox window.

As the ladies jostled for a good position, they set off a jaunty hanging sign sporting the cheery words, "It's a Good Day to Read a Book." The movement, in turn, disrupted a cluster of jolly miniature Santas placed atop the sign. Knocked off kilter, they tumbled down and hung precariously, trapeze-style, by their big black boots.

No one cared a jot about toppling Santas because, with noses pressed against the glass and hot breath misting up the windows, they were just able to make out the rotund figure of Mrs. Barber as she disappeared into the hairdresser's at the far end of the street.

The ladies of the book club unpeeled their faces from the steamed-up glass. The Labette twins, dressed impeccably and identically, as usual, in smart black pants and soft blue cashmere cowl-necked sweaters, were the first to speak.

"Well, I never," exclaimed Lottie in her extended southern drawl, and her sister, Lavinia, finished her sentence for her: "That can't be good. Maybe they forgot to remove all the color solution from her hair or something? I mean, why race to the hairdressers' like that? It can't be for a cut and blow dry, now can it?"

The twins looked much younger than their sixtyish years and had always been reluctant in admitting exactly which number followed the six. Yet aside from their age and appearance, they couldn't have been more different if you'd picked two people from the farthest corners of the planet. Charlotte, who was known as Lottie, had found Jesus at a revival meeting at the age of fourteen, while Lavinia had found James Rye and had her first French kiss behind the tent as the zealous, frothed-up preacher made his desperate altar call.

"You know, something like that happened to a friend of our mama's," said Lottie in a hushed tone as the ladies made their way back and retrieved their abandoned books. "Years ago, when we lived in Texas, my mama's friend had the most beautiful waist-length blonde hair and had gone in for a permanent. The girl at the Roller Up and Dye had left her under the dryer while she popped out to get herself a Coke. Anyway," continued Lavinia, "then she met this cute guy who worked down the street at the bakery, and they got to talking, and the girl clean forgot about Mama's friend. When she finally remembered to go back to remove her from the dryer, her hair had fried!"

Lavinia paused for effect, allowing a communal intake of breath before continuing the story.

"As she took out the rollers one by one, her beautiful blonde hair came out with them. Just odd sprigs were left here and there. She looked like a platinum-colored porcupine. It put a scare into everyone in our little town—as nobody wanted to go about looking like bleached woodland creatures—and the Roller up and Dye went out of business because of it."

"So it just rolled up and died, then?" I commented sarcastically as I picked up a pile of books. My humor was lost on the group.

"Exactly," answered Lottie. "I hope that doesn't happen to Sadie's. I do love that little hairdresser's."

"I don't think anything like that has happened," I responded practically as I moved about the library, humming to the Christmas music and shelving books. "Besides, her hair wasn't even wet. Something else must have happened."

Wearing her favorite purple leisure suit, Annie, the dog lover and continuous knitter of the group, stopped casting on, her ruddy red face suddenly coming to life. Always the optimist, she gushed, "I think it must be something wonderful. Maybe someone won the lottery, and she's rushing to let them know."

As the group stared blankly at their pages of Charlotte Brontë's classic novel, the earlier conversation of nineteenth-century love was gone and replaced by this new village anomaly.

Ruby-Skye, a radical hippie chick in her seventies, jumped to her feet and paced, jangling the abundance of bangles that completed her dramatic, eclectic style. She floated about the library in a yellow caftan cinched at the waist with a thick belt that resembled enormous banana leaves, her hair piled up like a pineapple, crested by a plume of multicolored feathers and dotted with dried oranges and lemons. Along with her signature bangles, the handmade jewelry that adorned her arms looked as if it had been made out of twigs and string. She called this ensemble Rainforest Mash-Up, whenever anyone asked her.

Suddenly, she clapped her hands.

"I do remember seeing Mrs. Barber run before!" she

exclaimed. "Our postmistress once took home the prize for second place in the three-legged race at the Fourth of July parade in 1971. I know because I was first!"

"That must have been the year before she sprouted those enormous bosoms," said Lavinia. "And that put an end to her three-legged career and her 1972 comeback. Mind you," she continued, "I bet they come in handy for swimming—more buoyancy than one of those noodles."

"Here she comes again," I shouted, having kept one eye on the window as I began rebalancing the dangling Santas.

"Go, Lorraine!" cried Lavinia, pumping the air with her fist as if cheering on a marathon runner.

Down with a unified clatter went *Jane Eyre* again as the ladies jumped to their feet and resumed their places at the letterbox window, moving back through the library in the opposite direction.

"Oh, bless her heart," added Lottie. "Someone should put a number on her back and have her raise money for cancer or something."

"She has someone with her!" I noted, screwing up my eyes, having left my place at the check-in desk to join the ladies traveling back through the handicraft section.

"Oh, is it Santa?" asked Annie excitedly.

"No, more like the Grinch," said Lavinia flatly. "Isn't that Doris? Our Doris Newberry?"

As the women drew closer to the window, Ruby-Skye, unabashed, pulled back the lace curtain hanging there as they all continued to peer out and watch the sprinters race up Main Street. Doris Newberry was the leader of the Rejected Writers' Book Club and chose not to join them for their forays into nineteenth-century England. She preferred more to write than to read.

Doris had formed the book club a few years before to celebrate being rejected by publishers in style. Each member brought her own rotten manuscripts to share with the group and then collected rejection letters from publishers like fan mail.

As we tried to get a clear view of the elf's accomplice, Lavinia remarked that she was definitely Doris's build and wore the same brown wool sweater she liked to wear, but it was hard to be sure as her hair was affixed with silver foil and white goo.

As we made our way back through the history section, it was confirmed: behind Mrs. Barber, Doris Newberry was now running back up Main Street, her hair in foil and with one of Sadie's mulberry-colored salon towels pinned and flapping in the breeze about her shoulders.

"Someone must be dead," said Lottie, a sudden apprehension in her tone.

"Surely they wouldn't run to the post office?" I reasoned. "Surely she would run home or to the police station?"

"Nope, something's going on, and we need to find out what," decided Lavinia.

"Yes, I shall never be able to concentrate on Mr. Rochester's proposal to Jane until I know exactly what this is all about," added Lottie.

It was decided we would go over en masse to find out for ourselves. It was a quiet day in the library, so I decided to tag along. Like a parade of ducks, we followed each other across the street and into the post office.

Doris was easy to spot: she looked like a rabid extraterrestrial with a mass of white bubbly solution and bits of foil sprouting out of her head. Some foil envelopes had worked themselves loose and dangled at the end of strands of sticky hair, rolling pendulum-like around the mulberry-colored towel, now smeared with the goo. She hunched across the post office counter, her head down as she read a letter in her hand, and Mrs. Barber nodded by her side.

"Is everything OK, Doris?" I asked, breaking the silence.

Doris threw back her hair, sending loose, fluffy gobs of color solution about the post office like wispy egg whites whipped up by an overzealous chef. She hurriedly folded the letter that Mrs. Barber had been reading from the counter and put it into her pocket.

"Oh . . . I . . . girls," she said in an overfriendly, high-pitched manner that sounded very unfamiliar coming from Doris's lips. "How nice to see you all."

"Nice to see you!" responded Lavinia. "We thought someone had had a cardiac arrest over here the way the two of you were running up and down the street."

Mrs. Barber reddened and mumbled something about sorting packages as she headed off very sheepishly back behind her desk.

Before Doris could elaborate, she was let off the hook by her hairdresser, Sadie, who appeared breathlessly at the door, a small timer in her hand.

"Doris Newberry!" she said as she leaned against the door-frame, puffing in and out, catching her breath. "What are you doing? I told you I was going back to sort that delivery of hair solutions, and when I came back, the timer was going off, and you were nowhere to be seen! It was like an alien abduction. The place was empty, and that solution needs to come out of your hair unless you're planning on being a twinkle light for Christmas. I have been looking in every shop up and down the high street. If it hadn't been for Karen Shaw at the library, I wouldn't even know where you were!"

Ruby-Skye folded her hands across her chest. "Well, are you going to tell us what's going on?" she asked.

Doris looked resolute.

"And why were you running up and down the street like someone was dead?" asked Lavinia of Mrs. Barber, who now stood puffing and blowing behind the counter.

"Important post office business," she said smartly.

"How important can it be when it's snail mail?" added Lottie.

"I had to make sure that Her Eminence got the information," responded Mrs. Barber.

"Her *what-enance*?" I asked with a smirk.

"Oh, I've said enough," said Mrs. Barber, and she disappeared into the back room.

We all turned to face Doris.

"Is there something you want to tell us?" I asked. "Something that your obedient servant over there wasn't able to divulge?"

Doris stiffened. "I will tell you in good time. It's a very wonderful surprise for Flora, something that she would never in a million years believe could happen."

I smiled to myself; I knew Doris had been driving Flora mad as a self-appointed "wedding coordinator." Having watched Flora's frustration with Doris's need to dominate every part of the wedding over the last few weeks, I knew that having Doris take a vacation would be the one thing that she'd be the most excited to have happen.

"I promise I'll reveal all in the right time, but I want to tell Flora myself," continued Doris. "Now, I need to get on. I have to get this goo out of my hair." She pushed past us toward the door.

"No problem, *Your Eminence*," responded Lavinia with both eyebrows raised. "We'll look forward to an audience with you at a different time."

And with that, Doris blew out of there. We walked back over to the library, and the women settled back at their table. Ruby shook her head. "I don't know what it is, but *whatever* it is—I have a feeling we're not going to like it."

～

BEHIND THE COUNTER of the local florist, All Stems from Here, the bride herself was poring over a wedding magazine at the counter and enjoying time before the flower shop opened at ten. Flora had been arriving at nine thirty all week, enjoying flipping through flower catalogs at her leisure so she could decide on the perfect shade of pink for her roses. This morning she had treated herself to a shiny, fat wedding magazine while she hummed along to classical Christmas music and sipped her peppermint tea. She skimmed through, looking for anything with a Victorian theme. Defying people of her own age, she dressed in and loved anything of that time period and rebelled against technology; she was barely able to use her iPod.

Suddenly, her heart jumped when someone rapped on the window of the shop. When she saw it was Dan, her fiancé, the usual butterflies found their way from her stomach to her chest. She couldn't believe he could still do that to her after being together for over two years.

She moved quickly to open the door. As soon as she unlocked it, his tall frame surrounded her with a huge bear hug. He wore the blue shirt she had bought him, and his dark, thick, curly hair was newly washed and still damp. She melted into his arms, enjoying the smell of his hair, clean from the shower. She nuzzled her cheek into his warm neck as she inhaled deeply his fresh, woody scent.

"What are you doing here?" she mumbled into his neck as he stroked and kissed her hair.

He pulled her back and looked at her, his emerald-green eyes intently gazing over her face as if it were for the first time. She didn't know how he could do that—always look at her as if he had never met her before and that somehow she was the most beautiful woman in the world.

"I was on my way to work, and I just needed to see you. Sometimes, Flora, I find it hard to believe that you're real and we're going to do this. Can you believe that in just a few weeks, we'll be married?"

Flora giggled and pulled him into the shop.

"You goofball," she said. "Won't you get into trouble? Aren't you supposed to be at work at ten?"

He smiled and kissed her warmly on the lips. Opening his eyes, he nodded. "Yep. It was worth it."

She pulled herself free of his arms, saying, "It won't be if you lose that job. Jones's is the only garage in town. You're lucky that his son decided to take that trip around the world so you could replace him as the mechanic over there. I would hate for you to lose it."

"OK," he said, "but I might need another hug around lunchtime. Can you meet over at the Crab for a sandwich?"

Someone rattled the front door of the shop.

Flora looked at the clock. It was two minutes past ten. Taking her fiancé's hand, she walked him to the door.

"Now go," she said. "I will try to get some time off, but I have to work now, and so do you."

She unlocked the door, let in the mother and the preschooler with a *good morning*, and gently nudged Dan out the door. He bent to brush her lips with one last kiss and was gone. As she watched him leave, her heart sank and she suddenly felt very alone. She flipped the sign on the door to "Open."

It had been hard making the decision not to live together before the wedding. Everyone had expected it, even encouraged it. But Flora, always traditional, loved the idea of leaving her home as a bride, marrying Dan, and moving in together. That would be their wedding present to each other. There'd been the usual warning of, "You don't really know someone until you live with them," from many people, but she wanted to wait. Otherwise, it felt like opening a present before Christmas. She knew there would be an adjustment, but she wanted that to be part of their newly married life. She was going to be with Dan for the rest of her life, no matter what people said about the pitfalls.

She moved back to her catalogs and smiled. Her tiny cottage in their town would never have been big enough for the two of them to live in, anyway. It had been her individual home for many years, and it just didn't seem right to change all that, even though she would've adored waking up with Dan every morning. She wanted to give herself time to look forward to that. And in a matter of weeks, they would move into a lovely, sunny, yellow-and-white home overlooking the water—a home of their own. She squealed with joy. Just a few short weeks and she would be Mrs. Flora Cohen.

$\approx$

As I ARRIVED home from working at the library that evening, Martin was waiting for me in the kitchen with a smile on his face.

"We have visitors coming," he said in a singsong way.

"We do?" I asked, clapping my hands with glee.

"Poopy and Dribble are making a comeback," he added, referring to our sweet grandbabies. "Time to tie down the toilet seat and batten all the hatches."

It had been quite an eventful eighteen months since my daughter, Stacy, had given birth to her twins, James and Olivia, whom Martin insisted on calling Poopy and Dribble.

I had been there for the emergency delivery, which was assisted by a singing teacher and all the Rejected Writers at Annie's farm in the woods, in the middle of a thunderstorm. Stacy's twins had arrived with much fanfare during one of the worst windstorms our island had ever had.

Martin handed me a cup of tea.

I looked around my Laura Ashley–style little blue kitchen. Our cottage wasn't really spacious enough to house rambunctious toddlers, and our cat, Raccoon, seemed to disappear for days when they arrived. But I couldn't wait.

"When are they coming?" I asked.

"In a couple of weeks. Stacy wants them to have plenty of time to practice being the flower girl and the ring bearer for the wedding."

I was warmed by the thought but also trying to picture these two balls of energy somehow tamed down enough to be out in public without killing themselves or anyone else.

My mind started whirring. "What do we need to get ready?" I said. "There are so many things to organize and do."

"First, *Grandma*," Martin said, settling me down in the chair, "we have to figure out where I'm going to go on vacation for a week while you gals are having a ball."

"Oh no you don't," I said in my warning tone. "This is what you signed up for when we decided to have Stacy."

He smiled broadly. "I only signed up for one baby. Is it my fault she decided to have two at a time?"

I chided him as I punched him gently on the arm. "Well, twins don't run in my family, so I think that gives you some responsibility, and the only ball you are going to see is a football. Apparently, James loves to play."

"At least with him only being eighteen months, I have a chance of winning," he said thoughtfully.

"Don't be so sure," I snipped back. "I've seen you play!"

CHAPTER TWO

PEAS IN RAIN BONNETS & WELCOME TO HICKSVILLE

A light, feathery rain started to fall on Washington early the next morning and continued right through into the late evening. Though insignificant in volume, it still had the ability to work its way down collars and up sleeves and soak its way into children's socks and shoes, seeping through fabric in search of exposed skin until it drenched to the very core.

The Labette twins, aware of this Northwest phenomenon, were both tightly laced into identical transparent rain bonnets and sat like two peas in a pod stretched under plastic. They stared blankly out of the car window through the dismal weather, having just returned from their off-island clothes-shopping expedition. They had spent the whole day looking for dresses to wear to Flora and Dan's wedding.

The Washington State car ferry powered down its engines and pulled in closer to the shore, and a horn blared to inform the occupants they had indeed arrived at the south end of the island. The engines slowed to a low rumble. Lavinia put away a fashion magazine she had been reading as Lottie hummed absently in tune to a Dolly Parton song playing on their radio.

A blast of wind picked up from the shore and whipped up

wayward raindrops that splattered haphazardly across the windowpane, and Lottie, who was staring out, transfixed, sighed. Being from the south, neither one of them cared much for the rain, even this delicate, wispy variety. It wasn't the rain itself, for Texas had its own share of weather from time to time, but the incessant, continuous presence of it they had to endure through the winter season that still, after all this time, overwhelmed them.

Lavinia had had to have a lesson on how to put on rain gear, for goodness sake. She remembered to this day the very first rain she saw fall on the town when they'd arrived, back in the 1970s. Lavinia thought about that now as she listened to her sister hit a crescendo in "Coat of Many Colors." She had cried when their poppa brought her up from Texas to escape a rather unfortunate third husband with a shotgun and a death wish. They had hightailed it out of town in the middle of the night, heading for the end of the earth, and this was the place they had ended up: a tiny island hidden in the top corner of the Pacific Northwest. Back then she'd thought she and Lottie would never survive a Northwest winter. Wearing every one of their clothes in layers that first year, they were soon introduced to the benefits of fleece and thick woolens. Now they had lived here for so long, she couldn't even remember a winter that wasn't gray.

The ferry lurched a little as it found its mooring, and in front of the sisters' sleek silver-blue Cadillac, a group of ferry workers in Santa hats bustled to life, pulling ropes and securing chains.

"I do love a boat ride," said Lottie as she took the prayer book from her lap and placed it into her bag.

Lavinia started the car in response to the ferry workers, who beckoned her to move forward. She slid gracefully into drive and made her way off the boat and then slowly up the hill. Behind her, a guy in a brown Pinto, obviously frustrated with Lavinia's pace, slammed his car into second, roared up the hill, and cut her off, almost clipping the side of her car. Lavinia swore a choice cussword that she kept for such occasions like this, and Lottie looked at her in horror, exclaiming, "Lavinia!"

"He deserved it," she responded tartly.

"But did I?" asked Lottie. "Mine are the only ears that can hear it. You may as well have called me that awful thing."

"Lottie, don't be so dramatic. A little cussword now and again keeps my blood flowing. Besides, I bet you thought it."

"I did no such thing," said Lottie as she continued to blink at her sister in disbelief. "I'll pray for that unfortunate young man."

Lavinia chuckled as she looked across at her sister. "You were the wholesome side of Mama's egg, Lottie, that is for sure."

THE GUY in the brown Pinto pulled into a spot outside of what appeared to be the only food store in town. He turned off the engine and looked at himself in the mirror. He had at least a day's worth of beard growth and his eyes were bloodshot, but he was here. He tried to think of a name that he'd call himself in this town—maybe David or Nick, something forgettable should work. He settled on his grandfather's name: John. He stepped out into the chilly, damp air and lit a cigarette as he leaned against his car.

He looked around at this quaint Northwest town and shook his head. Up and down the street, cedar wreaths hung from every lamppost and strings of multicolored Christmas lights adorned the trees. Across the street a group of people gathered in the tiny town square to watch carol singers wearing full Victorian costumes and carrying candles that flickered in tiny hooked lanterns.

John shook his head in disbelief. *So, this is Southlea Bay,* he thought to himself. He noticed that the store where he was parked was called the Twinkle and the doorway had been elaborately decorated for the season. A sign hanging from the door apologized for being closed. Under the official sign, a hand-written note with a smiley face announced to their customers that they had won the best-dressed Christmas shop doorway competition. He scoffed at the overly made-up entrance, with its thick white garland and an effusion of silver bows, white turtle-doves, and bells. He had been hoping to get some more cigarettes, but everywhere seemed to be closed. He looked at his phone; it was only nine p.m. What kind of a hick town shuts down at nine?

Outside the store, racks of tiny potted Christmas flowers were left unlocked and unattended. The owner apparently trusted that when he returned the following day, all his poinsettias would still be there.

John took a long, slow drag from his cigarette, savoring the nicotine as it filled his lungs and made him feel a little light-headed. An older guy walking a dog nodded at him and bid him *good evening.* For a minute, it took him off guard. John just managed a bob of his head in acknowledgment before the walker slipped by, his golden retriever trotting at his side. *That's right,* he thought, *in small towns, people speak to strangers.* He pulled his coat around his shoulders and shuddered. This kind of place made him nervous. He felt exposed and vulnerable. He preferred the gritty streets of any big city. The grime and hustle suited him so much more than these open, friendly towns, where they could leave a pot of flowers out and had to acknowledge every person who passed by.

John looked up at the streetlight. He could now see the driz-zling rain that was falling. It was so light that he had hardly noticed it, though it had already caused his cigarette and hair to dampen. He took one last full, deep drag, then threw his cigarette down and ground it into the asphalt with his heel. He got back into his car and pulled out his iPhone so he could map the place he needed to go to. It wasn't far, and a friend of a friend, who had moved from his town a year ago, had offered him a couch to sleep on and some casual work while he got settled.

John hadn't had the heart to tell him that settling was the last thing he planned to do in Southlea Bay. Once he found the girl he was looking for, he'd be gone before the guy had a chance to give him his mailing address. He started his car, put it in gear, and checked the address on his phone. With a squeal of his tires, he spun out of the parking lot, disappearing up the Main Street hill in a blast of choking blue fumes.

CHAPTER THREE

NEON WAITRESSES & BACKCOMBED POODLES

As I made my way home from the library on Saturday morning, I noticed Flora's thoroughly miserable expression through the window of the Bob and Curl Hair Salon. I shook my head, thinking, *I bet she wishes she hadn't mentioned at last week's Rejected Writers' Book Club meeting that she had planned to talk to Sadie about possible styles for her wedding.* Because now, as she sat in one of Sadie's black leather-and-chrome chairs, looking in the large cream-colored framed mirror, eight faces were staring back at her.

I opened the door and noted that Sadie, our local hairdresser, had been momentarily called away to answer a ringing phone. I approached the station Flora was sitting at and added my face to the bouquet already reflected in the mirror just in time to hear the formidable leader of our group speak.

"What about a color?" Doris said as she pursed her lips and swung the swivel chair toward her. She then grabbed a chunk of Flora's hair and scrutinized it an inch from her nose. "Maybe copper or red—it's so dull and pale."

"Oh no," I said, rubbing Flora on the shoulder. "I'm sure Dan loves Flora's *blonde* hair just the way it is." I emphasized the word *blonde* to reassure Flora, then continued, "Besides, her natural color will look lovely with the delicate pink roses she's planning to trim her veil with."

Our sweet bride-to-be, who was barely in her twenties, could often feel overwhelmed by this group of eccentric middle-aged women. She was, I knew, already self-conscious of her very pale features, rice-paper skin, and delicate bone structure that was more the epitome of a classic Alma Tada art piece than a Kardashian.

Flora smiled awkwardly as I caught a glimpse of Ruby-Skye.

Our eccentric hippie squinted her eyes, as if she were visualizing a whole new look for Flora. "Cut it all off, Flora, you'd be so cute with a pixie." She jumped down from where she'd been perched on the top of one of the hairdressing stations. Taking both sides of Flora's hair, she scrunched it in her hands to just under Flora's chin, making it look like hardly any hair was left. But Ruby-Skye was now in full flow. "With your great bone structure and lovely eyes, a short cut with strong, dramatic lines would just look stunning under your veil."

The outcry from the rest of the ladies made it obvious no one else agreed with this suggestion.

"A girl can't go down the aisle with no hair!" Lavinia snapped as she took Ruby-Skye's place behind Flora's chair. "It's our one true beauty. And Flora has such a lovely full head of hair." Taking hold of Flora's hair, she ran her hands backward through it until it fluffed up like a teased cotton ball. "I would say, go big, Flora. Lots of curls and bounce." She continued to backcomb and tease Flora's hair with her fingers. "Why, for my second wedding, I did just that. I don't regret it; it was stunning. I had a hundred fresh rosebuds and pearl beads sown in all the way through it. Though, to be honest, the hairstyle lasted longer than my new husband's fidelity." She pursed her lips. "I found him out back of the wedding reception venue, fraternizing with one of my bridesmaids, if you know what I mean."

Ethel, the quietest and most prudish of the group, blinked twice behind her metal-rimmed spectacles, her eyes growing as large as saucers in the mirror at Lavinia's confession.

As I looked at Flora's hair, piled up like a puffy white pompom, I couldn't help but wonder if Flora was beginning to know how a show poodle might feel.

"You're making her look like an ice-cream sundae," Gracie, the oldest member of the group, said and then giggled. "It's making me hungry." Doris's momma, who was well into her nineties and loved playing dress up, wore her signature pink feather boa and red-and-white polka dot rain boots.

"Real rosebuds," retorted Doris to Lavinia. "That is ridiculous. It's her hair, not a garden. It should be a nice, practical chignon or a bun." With that, Doris pulled back Flora's now doubled-in-volume hair into a bun off her face so tightly that Flora's skin tightened till her eyes were practically slits.

Annie stopped knitting for a minute to take in Flora's disappearing hairline and stretched skin. "I think Flora looks fine as she is," she said with a confirming nod. "I have always loved her hair long, flowing straight down her back."

Sadie, the woman who ran the Bob and Curl, returned to her station. Now back at her chair, she took control.

"Now girls," she said, taking Flora's hair gently from Doris's clawlike grip, "give poor Flora a chance to breathe and think. She's never going to be able to make up her mind with all of you clucking around her like a bunch of mother hens. Why don't you let me get out my wedding book and spend some time with Flora alone first?"

As she talked, she gently combed Flora's flyaway hair out of its mangled nest and smoothed it down her back. Flora's expression relaxed as Sadie continued, "Why don't you go to the Crab Apple for coffee and come back later, when we may have more ideas. I'm sure Flora would appreciate your opinion when she's made up her own mind of the direction she wants to go in." Sadie spoke in an assured and tactful way that proved she'd dealt with her fair share of mothers, sisters, and helpful friends of the bride.

All the ladies stood frozen until Sadie shooed them with her hands.

I turned to follow the ladies out the door, but before I got to it, Flora grabbed my arm.

"Thank you both," she said looking from me to Sadie, the relief obvious in her voice. "You have no idea."

"Don't you worry, Flora," said Sadie, tapping her on the arm. "I've dealt with lots of mothers of the bride before. Never seven at a time, mind, but they have their hearts in the right place. The first thing you need to realize about getting married is that everyone loves a wedding, and somehow that makes them all feel they have a stake in it. If you thought this was just about you and Dan, think again. Weddings are a big deal, especially yours, in particular. They've all seen you grow up, and with the loss of your parents, they all feel a responsibility to you. I'm going to make it fabulous. We're going to start by creating the perfect hairstyle, one you feel comfortable with. So first things first: I'll get you a cup of tea, and I will get my wedding book." She patted Flora's hand. "And Flora, you're safe with me."

Flora smiled, took a deep breath, and relaxed.

"You're right." Her eyes shone as she smiled at my reflection in the mirror. "My wedding is going to be amazing—I can feel it. I can't wait to marry Dan."

I nodded and smiled back reassuringly before exiting the salon to make my way to the diner. As I walked the short distance to join the others, I contemplated everything I had to deal with living in a tightknit community. It sure was different to California where I had lived before.

I joined Annie, Doris, Ethel, the Labettes, and Gracie at the Crab. It was Saturday morning, and there was already a large crowd gathered in the foyer. But even back by the door and with a mass of people ahead of us, I could already see Gladys, the diner's most notorious waitress, behind her welcome desk. That was because she was luminous—literally. Her usual plain brown hair was bright pink. And not a sweet, gentle pink—more like cerise.

When we finally got to the front of the queue, Gladys threw her eyes to the ceiling and clicked her tongue, not even trying to hide her disapproval of our group as we all stared at the beacon of neon light on top of her head. Before one of us could speak, she sucked in her breath, hitched up her pantyhose, and said, "Before any of you ask, my goddaughter did it. She's making her way through beauty school and needed a victim to practice on. The girl she'd chosen had just broken up with her boyfriend and couldn't make it to her color class, so I stepped in last minute. She wanted me to choose one of those lame colors, like mahogany or burgundy, but I said if we're gonna dye it, let's make a statement. I always liked pink, so I said, 'Hit me up.'"

"It's very. . . um, nice," I said eventually. "Bright and cheerful."

"Well, I think it looks ridiculous," snapped Doris. "You look like cotton candy."

"Oh good," Gladys snapped back. "My favorite food."

Knowing there was history between Gladys and Doris, I stepped forward and used my most pleasant voice to ask for a table.

"For all of you?" scoffed Gladys. "Where are we squeezing into today, the bunker booth, where you can plot your next crazy road trip? Or are we back in the forest next to the bathroom, where you can dance around and create your next great Broadway musical?"

"We have very important business to discuss. Very important business indeed," Doris stated over my head sharply. Ethel, by her side, nodded her approval.

Gladys raised her eyebrows in disbelief. "Of course you do, Homeland Security is waiting on you to update the president. Let me see if the briefing room is ready."

Grabbing a stack of menus, Gladys shuffled back through the restaurant, the whole group of us in tow like a line of bewildered day-trippers following behind our glowing tour guide. As she went, she mumbled under her breath, "Why can't you come in on Mondays and Fridays? I'm off on those days!"

"Because we love to torture you," I joked.

Gladys stopped and gave me the hairy eyeball. Then she slowly circled us twice around the restaurant like a middle-aged circus procession. On the second lap, I fought the urge to smile and wave or hand out candy. Maybe her thinking was if she walked us around long enough, a table would become free or, better still, she would lose us along the way. We ended up back at the front of the restaurant. Finding two smaller tables that could be put together, she glared at Doris.

"Will this do, your ladyship?"

Doris sniffed, then reluctantly nodded. "It'll have to."

Gladys placed both hands on the table and shunted it at a snail's pace until it joined with the other table.

We all sat down, and Gladys slapped menus in front of each of us, saying, "I'll be back when I've had a Valium."

A busboy arrived at the table and gave us unsure glances. We had never really lived down the rumors that we were just a bunch of cougars after one of the young busboys, even though we'd just been looking for chorus members for our musical show. The sandy-haired boy approached the table, biting his lip.

"It's OK," I said, tapping his hand. "You don't have to sing for us today. All we want is water." His face broke into a nervous grin, as if he didn't like the fact that his thoughts had been read. With his hand shaking slightly, he filled up our water glasses.

Ruby-Skye arrived after checking on the emporium. Today she looked like she was wearing some sort of a cocktail dress made of sequins, and her hair was still up in a pineapple-shaped style, scattered with even more fruit. "We've got to make it fast," she said. "I have a huge wool event that I'm organizing over at my store."

Gladys shuffled back to the table and looked Ruby up and down. "Oh goody, Carmen Miranda has been raised from the dead."

Ruby-Skye patted her hair with her hand, ignoring her.

As soon as we finished ordering, Doris didn't waste any time letting us know what was on her mind.

She leaned forward and said the word in a very pronounced way: *"Shower."*

We all stared back blankly.

"Do you need one or are you expecting one?" asked Lavinia as she looked out of the window, confused.

"Flora's," Doris added.

"Oh, I do love wedding showers," said Lottie.

"I remember all of mine," added Lavinia. "My first one was so sweet. All my friends came to that one. By the third shower, we were lucky if we could get family members to attend. But as it was a shotgun wedding, nobody seemed that excited about it—apart from the guys with the shotguns, of course."

Ethel stopped sipping her water and once again blinked at Lavinia. It seemed that the twins' need to overshare was obviously hitting all of her buttons today.

"I have big plans," said Doris. "Big plans indeed."

I shuddered. These were always the words I dreaded the most. The last two times she'd had *big plans*, first, I'd ended up on a wild road trip, and then the second time, directing her crazy musical.

"But I want to keep it a surprise for Flora," she added in a hushed tone. "I have a list of ideas, but this is my favorite." She laid out pictures of African animals on the table.

"Are we riding them or eating them?" asked Lavinia distrustfully.

"Neither," said Doris. "We're wearing them."

"I'm not sure I will look very good as a zebra," said Lottie.

"I will not wear real fur, you know that," added Ruby sternly.

"No one has to wear any animals," said Doris with annoyance. "They have plenty of synthetic stretchy material with spots and stripes over at the fabrics store."

"Why are we wearing zebras and giraffes?" I asked, trying not to show my lack of enthusiasm. However, Gracie's eyes positively glowed at the prospect as Doris continued.

"I was thinking of an African-themed party for her bridal shower. We could even go mad and stage it at the zoo, if you want."

Annie stopped knitting and knotted her eyebrows. "Somehow I can't see Flora running around in a monkey cage in a bearskin. It sounds very un-Flora-like."

It sounded very "un-sane"-like to me.

"I have bongo drums," said Doris. "I've started playing drums for exercise. We could all do that and wear leopard skins and animal costumes. I could even wear my beaver coat."

"I don't think beavers are in the jungle," said Lavinia tartly.

"I was going to do something with it," said Doris defensively. "Make it look like a deer or something."

"I don't think there are deer in Africa, either," said Lottie as she sipped her tea.

"Well, any old African beasts will do," said Doris losing patience.

Those were the words Gladys heard as she came back to the table to get our order.

"Old African beast," she repeated pulling a pencil from her usual bra cubbyhole and the curled-up notepad that also sat in the same place. "I think African beast is off today, but we've got a nice piece of veal."

Ruby-Skye slammed her hand down on the table. "I can't believe you guys are carrying veal. Have you any idea how that is prepared? I absolutely protest. Whom can I complain to?"

"Well, not me," said Gladys, adjusting her bosom. "I only work here, so stop your crabbing and I'll get you a manager. Oops, he's not here today, so you'll have to complain tomorrow, when I have the day off." Gladys took our orders and shuffled off to do our bidding.

"What else is on the list?" asked Ruby. I could see she was very unimpressed with the wedding shower on the Serengeti.

I looked at the list Doris had placed on the table with the pictures of wildebeest that were still wandering across it. I read out option number two: "Fairies."

"That was my idea," said Gracie, lighting up. "I thought we could do a fairy tea party, maybe in the woods. Wouldn't that be fun? I have the perfect costume for it. We could all dress as woodland folk."

I squinted at Doris, who was a very rotund, heavyset woman with a perpetually stern expression. Seeing her dressed as a fairy was not in the realm of my imagination.

"Why do we have to have a theme at all?" asked Lottie. "I mean, we could just turn up and have some snacks and some drinks, give out gifts and maybe have a couple party games."

Doris slammed down her piece of paper on the table. "We have to have a theme. All the best people have a theme. This is Flora's wedding. We've got to do it right. She's only gonna get married once."

"I don't think fairies are it," said Lottie, shaking her head, obviously also trying to imagine Doris in a glittery tutu. "I think my fairy days are gone. I haven't wanted to be any kind of wood-land creature or a witch since the last endeavor that you put me through. I think my hips are still out from being raised up and down on that wire during that musical show."

"What about some sort of Victorian party?" said Annie thoughtfully. "What about one of Flora's favorite stories, like *Pride and Prejudice* or *Sense and Sensibility*? She loves Jane Austen. Can't we have a Jane Austen–themed party?"

Everyone paused.

"Flora would love it," I said.

"What about my bongo playing?" said Doris. "Is there a Jane Austen story set in Africa? I think a combination would be perfect. We could call it African Jane Austen."

None of us were convinced. As much as we protested, Doris was not backing down.

"Now where shall we have it?" Doris pulled out her infamous clipboard.

"We could have it at our house," said Lottie. "We've got the space."

Doris balked. "What about my house? There's nothing wrong with my house."

"Well, no offense, honey," said Lottie, "but I'm not sure your . . . home has quite the right tone to set for Edwardian England." She said it carefully as we all pictured Doris's '70s furniture and white wicker décor. "And we do have a lot more room."

"We will be delighted to hold it at our house. We have the Jane Austen–esque sweeping staircase, and we could hire a butler for the night."

Doris was outvoted. She couldn't compete with a sweeping staircase and a butler.

"Next Thursday evening, then," said Lavinia with finality. "We will expect to see you ladies in your Edwardian attire—"

"Or African," added Doris.

Lottie sighed, echoing quietly, "Or African, if you feel so inclined."

"For our Christmas Edwardian Affair," proclaimed Lavinia.

We all nodded and started to eat.

～

JOHN PULLED into the parking lot of the Twinkle. He'd run out of cigarettes last night. As he entered the store, the sound of Bing Crosby singing "The Christmas Song" filled the air. John walked absently around the store, looking at packets of seasonal candy and colorfully foiled chocolate Santa's, and thought about how this reminded him of a '50s TV show. Shelves stacked with Christmas goodies and wholesome homemade, organic foods as local people gathered in aisles, making small talk about pets and children.

A clean-cut man, wearing an elf hat and a cheerful blue apron with the words *Happy to serve you* written across it, nodded at him. He was pricing peas as if he lived to label cans. John shuddered. He wasn't gonna last long in this town, he could tell. Thank goodness he didn't have to.

"Can I help you?" asked a fresh-faced young girl with a mass of frizzy red hair, a scrubbed complexion, and a nose dotted with freckles. He'd been stopped in front of the fridge while trying to get his bearings. She continued before he had time to answer. "The hummus is locally made, fresh and yummy," she added, smiling, pointing to a product in the fridge.

He looked at the tubs of cream goo and had no idea what they were. In fact, there were many things in the fridge he didn't know. He knew what seaweed was, of course—which he noticed was next to the hummus—but he couldn't imagine why anyone would want to eat it.

He broke into a full smile and his voice cracked, a result of drinking and smoking late into the night with his new friend. "Thanks," he said.

The girl walked away, saying over her shoulder, "Let me know if you need anything else from me."

A wicked thought crossed his mind as she left. He stopped himself and focused on what he was here for. He grabbed a Red Bull, walked back to the counter, and was greeted with another smile by the same checkout girl. She was chatting with a school-aged girl with long black hair, who was bagging groceries. He ordered cigarettes as they continued their conversation.

"I just saw Flora in the Bob and Curl," said the young girl at the counter.

The girl at the checkout almost swooned. "How cool, I hope she'll put it up for her wedding," she said. "She looks so elegant with her hair up."

John shifted his weight, intently interested.

"A wedding—nice," he blurted, trying to remember how to make small talk. He attempted to seem casual. It was hard work, but he was intrigued with what they had to say. He didn't want to draw attention, though, so he veered off on a different tact. "I really do need a haircut. The Bob and Curl, is that a hairdresser around here?"

He expected them to tell him to mind his own business, but they didn't seem at all put out by the fact that he'd asked such a direct question. In the city, they would have told him what to do with himself.

"Yes," the checkout girl said, giving him his cigarettes with one hand and taking his money with the other, "it's right across the street."

"Thanks . . . I really do need to get my hair cut."

"Of course," answered the bright-faced young thing as if she didn't seem weary of him at all. "Just past the Wool Emporium."

She grabbed his arm as he started to leave and he froze.

"Don't forget your free candy cane," she said, giggling and twirling a red-and-white peppermint stick in front of his face.

He took it from her reluctantly, offering a half-cocked smile that even he knew looked pathetic.

He walked out into the chilly morning, stuffed the candy cane into his pocket, pulled his jacket up around his ears, and lit a cigarette. He took a deep, long drag. He held the smoke in for a moment and then he let his breath out slowly. He walked across the parking lot toward the Bob and Curl, which he could now clearly see across the street.

He crept cautiously up to the window and looked in, standing back from view so he couldn't be seen. A woman sat in a chair—long pale-blonde hair, just as he had remembered seeing in the picture. A hairdresser had the young woman's hair in one hand as she looked at the magazine on her lap.

John smiled to himself. *This is going to be easy,* he thought as he continued to watch her until he'd finished smoking his cigarette. Then he made his way back to the car. All he needed now was to wait. He looked at his phone. He was starting a job and meeting his new boss in five minutes. This work would keep him going until he executed his plan. Then he would be out of here.

CHAPTER FOUR

FROLICKING FAIRIES & COUGAR
ENCOUNTERS

The following Thursday, the Labette sisters returned from buying party items for Flora's shower and drove in their silver-blue Cadillac the short distance to the edge of town, where they lived. Their home was one of the most beautiful in Southlea Bay. Perched high on the bluff, the French chateau–style house was one of a kind. Lavinia approached the tall black wrought iron gates that surrounded the property and pressed a number into the keypad. She took a breath as she waited for them to open. This kind of security wasn't really necessary in their sleepy little town, but Poppa had insisted on it just in case Hank somehow found her. It used to make her feel secure to see the tall wrought iron gates reassuring presence, but now, as she got older, it seemed like one big inconvenience. She drummed on the steering wheel as her sister looked out of the window.

"What a lovely day," remarked Lottie as the gates opened and the view of the Sound slipped into view. It was a stunning vista. The lawn rolled away to an expansive overlook of the water, with the frosted Cascades as its backdrop.

They glided down their long, looped driveway toward the elegant house they called home. It was far too big for the two of them, but they had lived there for forty years and hadn't the heart to downsize. Besides, Lavinia would often joke, "I still might want to have children. Women my age are doing it with egg donations all the time," just to make her sister blush. Lottie would undoubtedly say, "Lavinia!" in that exasperated way, which happened at least ten times a day.

Lavinia went inside while Lottie lingered in the driveway, taking a moment to enjoy the breath-taking view. All at once, she was struck with an idea. She couldn't believe she hadn't thought of it before.

"Lavinia! Lavinia! Come quickly."

Lavinia poked her head out of an upstairs window. "Are you yelling at me?" she snapped.

"I am," said Lottie. "Come down here at once."

Lavinia rolled her eyes, closed the window, and made her way down to her sister's side in the garden.

"I've had the most amazing idea," remarked Lottie excitedly.

"Don't tell me—you're going to plant petunias this year instead of marigolds."

"No, nothing like that." She grabbed her sister's arm and led her across their beautifully manicured lawn to a white clapperboard building that sat at the bottom of the garden on the edge of the bluff.

Lottie opened the hefty wooden doors and allowed the fresh air to seep into the vast musty room.

"Well?" said Lottie. "What do you think?"

"What do I think about what?" inquired Lavinia, peeking inside.

"The games room—what if we were to encourage Flora to have her wedding right here?"

"Why would Flora want to have her wedding in Poppa's old games room?" responded Lavinia, screwing up her face.

"I think it would be wonderful," continued Lottie. "She talked about having it in the community hall on the beach since the hotel she booked in town burned down. But it's so cold this time of year, and who needs all that sand in your salad? I think we should propose this."

"That's an interesting thought," responded Lavinia, nodding, looking around the room and starting to visualize it. "You might be on to something. We could pay a team to clean it up, and the view of the water is stunning."

They walked back through the room toward the door.

"Why don't we surprise Flora with it tonight? I think we could do a big reveal during the party. Don't get me wrong, the delicate intimates you bought are wonderful," said Lottie. "But I think this could be a fabulous gift."

Both sisters smiled, looked around the room, and nodded before walking out the door.

"They'll probably want to take pictures for the *Bay Breeze*," added Lottie wistfully as they made their way back across the lawn arm in arm.

Lavinia raised her eyebrows in a playful expression. "That would be a change. Normally the only reports about me in our local newspaper are scandals."

"Lavinia," screeched Lottie. She eyed her sister and shook her head. "You do tease me."

As they moved into the house, their doorbell chimed "Angels We Have Heard on High." Lottie had changed it especially for the season.

"Speak of the devil, here's an angel now," said Lavinia.

"I'll change into my gardening clothes," said Lottie. "Why don't you let him in?"

Lottie headed up the elegant staircase that dominated the hallway while Lavinia made her way to the door and the keypad that operated the gates.

"Hey there, Todd," she said, observing the landscaping truck on the screen.

"Hi there, Miss Lavinia," he answered. He never had a problem, like other folk, of telling them apart. "I'm here for your winter spruce-up."

She pressed a button on the keypad with her long pink fingernail and watched the gardening crew as they entered the property. Within a few moments, they were at the door. She opened it and greeted them.

"Lottie will be down in a moment to walk the property with you. We had a tree come down in last week's storm and . . ." Lavinia stopped midsentence as she spotted a young man on Todd's crew she hadn't met before. "Who is this handsome young fellow?" she said, gazing into his eyes and extending her hand.

Todd stepped back to introduce him. "This is a new guy we just got. He's a friend of one of our other workers."

The young man took Lavinia's hand gently, saying, as if butter wouldn't melt in his mouth, "I was just going to ask who this lovely woman was. I had been led to believe the ladies here were over twenty-one."

Lavinia chuckled and batted her eyelashes. "I know I'm going to like you," she said as her gaze lingered upon him. *He reminds me of one of my first boyfriends,* she thought. His sandy hair and blue eyes, along with his casual jeans and T-shirt, were very similar to her beau, Robert. He was older than Robert had been at the time, though, she mused. This young man looked to be in his early twenties, while she had dated Robert in high school. Just then, Lottie joined them at the door in her large gardening hat and gloves. "Lottie, we have a new man," enthused Lavinia.

Lottie smiled and bobbed her head in his direction.

"I didn't catch his name," said Lavinia.

"John, at your service," he responded without hesitation.

"I bet you are," said Lavinia playfully. They all laughed.

Lottie walked out to the garden as Lavinia waved after them.

"Have a good work day," she sang out. "And pleased to meet you, John. I'll see you later."

He looked back at her and smiled.

~

JOHN HAD BEEN WORKING for about two hours when he noticed Lavinia Labette heading out onto the patio at one o'clock that afternoon with a jug and a plate of cookies.

She placed her tray on the patio table and then called to Todd, who was pruning one of the trees across the lawn. Todd waved to her and shouted back, "I'll be there in a minute!"

It wasn't usual for people doing lawn service to be served tea, but Todd had informed John that the Labettes insisted on it. They had stipulated that if they didn't get to serve the men a drink, Todd's crew would no longer be able to work there. So Todd and his team had gotten used to doing just that in the last eight years. It was like a little ritual. They would drink their tea—or, as in this case, hot apple cider—while Lavinia fussed around them. It seemed to do more good for the sisters than for the team, Todd had assured him.

John put down his clippers. He'd been waiting for the tea call for the last thirty minutes. Now he'd have time to contrive his plan. He walked quickly to the table and beamed at Lavinia. He had spent a good deal of time that morning preparing himself: best green shirt, clean-shaven face, cologne.

"Why, you look chipper," purred Lavinia as she looked him over. "Almost good enough to eat."

He smiled, saying, "I could say the same about you, Ms. Labette." He looked Lavinia over. She wasn't bad-looking for her age: trim figure, cornflower-blue eyes, and only a streak of gray in her thick, dark hair.

Lavinia waved her hand in his direction. "Hush now. Call me Lavinia. Only my doctor calls me Ms. Labette."

"Well, I wouldn't want anyone to think that I'm that," he said with a grin.

He sat while she poured him a glass of the cider. She added a cinnamon stick and handed the glass to him.

He needed to be careful. He had done some investigating to find out more about the Rejected Writers' Book Club, and now he was ready to implement his plan. He looked out at the water and decided on just the right words. "Such a lovely garden," he said. "You must find it very inspirational for your writing."

Lavinia smiled and her whole face brightened. "Why, yes, I do," she said.

He tried to sound nonchalant. "I mention it because I write myself. Nothing major, just a detective novel, I've sent it out to a lot of publishers but nobody seems to want it . . ." He let his voice trail off. He didn't want to force it.

"I know what you mean," said Lavinia, taking off her hat and placing it on the table. "It's very difficult to get published. That's why I love my rejection group." She took in a deep breath.

He itched for a cigarette to calm his nerves, but he wanted to give her the impression of a sober and wholesome appearance. Focus. He needed to focus. He took a sip of his drink and tried not to balk at the taste of all the sugar she had added. After he swallowed it hard, he said, "Tell me more about your rejection group."

"Oh, hush," said Lavinia. "You don't want to know about a group of women getting together to read their stories. Why don't you tell me about where you come from and what brought you here?"

She fluttered her eyelashes.

John mopped at his brow with his sleeve. He hadn't had time to think of a good story for himself. She'd completely taken him off guard.

"I'm not very interesting," he mumbled. "I just came here looking for a new experience." He was thinking quickly. "Good for writing, gives me inspiration."

His mind whirred, his heart beating so fast he could hardly breathe. All he could think about was how badly he needed to smoke. When he had heard that the Labettes wrote books with

Flora, he thought it was going to be a lot easier than this. He hadn't been prepared for all these questions—for friendly, open people wanting to know who he was and where he was from.

Lavinia smiled and he saw that she noticed his hand was shaking. It appeared she seemed to think it was something to do with her presence, and she appeared to like it a lot. *Jeez,* he thought, *this is going from bad to worse.*

Suddenly, the opportunity was gone because two other landscapers arrived at the table and Lavinia went into full-on southern hospitality mode, fussing around them like a mother hen, fixing them cider and making them comfortable. Before he knew it, the time was up and he'd blown his chance to find out more about Flora. But as Lavinia was clearing the tray, she paused.

"Oh, Todd," she called after his boss, "I have a special meeting of my rejected ladies group at five p.m. We're going to surprise Flora with an idea to have her wedding here. Is there any chance you could just clip that tree at the south window? It looks ragged, and I want Flora to have a great view as she pictures how pretty it could be here."

Todd nodded. "No problem." He turned to John and pointed at the tree, sending him with clippers to take care of the job. As John moved across the lawn, he had another idea. He took of his hat, stuffed it behind the bushes, and started pruning the branches. Yes, this idea would work nicely. Maybe even better than the original plan.

≈

DORIS PACED AROUND HER KITCHEN, worrying. It was Thursday afternoon, the meeting day for the Rejected Writers' Book Club, which was usually at Doris's, but the Labettes were hosting this ridiculous bridal shower. As Doris busied herself around the kitchen while making lunch, she bristled at the thought. Lavinia had called that morning to remind her to be there early, as, apparently, they had a huge surprise for Flora.

Doris didn't really like surprises. They often didn't turn out well. What if the surprise was something Flora didn't like? There was nothing but anticipation and disappointment. This wasn't good. This wasn't good at all. As she finished up the dishes she was doing, her mama wandered into the kitchen, wearing a full-length nightie, a purple housecoat, and her polka dot rain boots. Her hair appeared to be windswept and damp.

Doris sighed. "Mama, what have you been doing in your nightclothes? I hope you haven't been outside."

It was evident by the twinkle in Gracie's eye that that was exactly where she'd been. She'd come to live with her daughter over a decade before, although her delicate, childlike features were so opposite of Doris's bulbous figure and large bones, it was impossible to believe they could be mother and daughter at all. Not just in looks but also in manners. Doris was apt to jump to the wrong conclusion and judge people quickly, whereas Gracie had all the time and patience of a child. Gracie walked over to a teapot that was being kept warm under a knitted tea cozy that Annie had made for them. She poured herself a cup of Earl Grey —her favorite tea—and smiled at her daughter.

"Oh, Dotty, you do worry far too much. I was just fixing a little angel sign that fell over in the flower beds. It was supposed to say 'Get Lost in the Magic of Nature,' and instead the words *Magic of Nature* dropped off and it just said 'Get Lost.'"

Doris cringed at her mother's use of her childhood name. It made Doris feel like she sounded unhinged in some way. She swallowed down her discomfort and said, "You shouldn't be wandering about outside like that. You could catch your death of cold. I do wish you wouldn't fuss with that pile of junk you keep out there."

Gracie took her time answering her daughter. She sat down at the table and removed her boots, took a long, slow sip of the tea, then explained, "The name for it is 'garden art,' and people are always commenting on how welcomed they feel when they arrive at our house." The *garden art* Gracie was referring to were dozens of signs, angels, and doodads all adorning their property with breezy sayings encouraging passers-by to have happy thoughts and a good day. Doris didn't have time for such trivialities, but Gracie insisted that she wouldn't come and live with Doris unless her little family of "happiness signs," as she called them, came right along with her. In addition to signs, she also had fairies and sprites and angels and frogs dotted about the garden, all cheerfully bobbing and waving.

Doris *humphed*. "*Garden art*" she pooh-poohed.

"What cake are you baking for the Rejected Writers tonight?" Gracie asked, changing the subject.

Doris stopped drying the dishes and sighed. "We've been invited to the Labette sisters' tonight, remember, Momma?" she reminded Gracie, unable to hide the disappointment in her voice.

But Gracie was upbeat. "Lovely. That'll be a nice change. Will they be serving tea and cake, do you think?"

Doris furrowed her brow. "I would think so," she said, but now she was concerned. She didn't want her standards dropping just because they'd moved the group to another house for the night. Maybe, to be on the safe side, she'd bake one and take it with her.

CHAPTER FIVE

AFRICAN JANE AUSTEN & POP-UP GROOMS

I arrived at the Labettes' stunning home at 5:30 p.m. for Flora's bridal shower. I got out of my car and stood in the driveway, taking in the gorgeous view. Because I had arrived so early, I was surprised to see Doris drive in behind me. We had all been told to wear our favorite Edwardian or Victorian outfit, so when I opened the car door for Doris, I was confused to find her wearing her beaver fur coat. Gracie was seated beside her, dressed as a fairy, and in the back seat, Ethel looked as if she was dressed as some sort of stern Amish woman. They looked like a bunch of kids who'd gotten lost in the rummage sale box.

"I thought this was a Jane Austen theme party?" I said, scrutinizing them.

"And African, remember?" Corrected Doris. "We said we could do both."

"I'm Elizabeth Bennett's fairy godmother," announced Gracie, waving her wand as she got out of the car. "I'm here to summon Flora's very own Mr. Darcy quicker than she can do it herself."

I smiled at Gracie, then nodded at Ethel.

"This was my mother's," she said stiffly, punctuating her

sentence in the sort of tone that didn't encourage any further deliberation.

Doris handed me a set of bongo drums and an enormous walnut cake. Neither of which said *bridal shower* or *Jane Austen* to me.

We made our way to the front door. I pressed the doorbell, and "Angels We Have Heard on High" chimed from within.

The person who opened the door wasn't Lavinia or Lottie, though. Instead, a tall man with dark hair loomed over us, wearing a traditional butler suit. "Good evening, ladies," he said with a perfect British accent. "Are the Mses. Labettes expecting you?"

Next to me, Ethel sucked in her breath, and I sensed she was contemplating hitching up her Amish petticoats and hightailing it out of there.

Gracie's eyes just sparkled. "Wow," was all she could say.

"Why, yes," I said, taking hold of Ethel's sleeve to stop her from making a run for it. "We're indeed here to see the two Labette sisters."

All at once, Lavinia was by his side, dressed in an elaborate Edwardian ball gown in burgundy silk, her hair piled up in a very elegant style.

"Good gracious," I said, feeling totally underdressed in my high-collared white blouse, cameo brooch, and long skirt I had once used for a circle-dancing foray in my younger days. "You know how to throw a party. You look stunning."

"Oh, we just went with 'Depressing *Gone with the Wind*,'" she responded, enthusiastically. "Believe it or not, we actually had these dresses hanging in our closets from an old Southern fundraiser party we had here years ago. I just Edwardian-ed it up, made it drearier and more dismal, just like their English weather," she added with a sweep of her hand.

"And who is this good-looking fella?" I said, nodding at the butler.

"This is Jeeves," said Lavinia coyly, squeezing his arm.

He slid back into his American accent for a moment. "Hi, my name's Brian," he said, offering me his hand. "I'm a local actor here on the island. The Labettes have hired me this evening to be their English help." He straightened up and gripped his lapel with his right hand. "How am I doing?" he added in a very austere British tone.

"Very well," I said. "I feel like I'm back in one of Jane Austen's books."

Doris huffed her disapproval behind me. As we moved into the hallway, Lottie joined her sister by her side, dressed identically.

"Where do you want me to stick this cake?" Doris grumbled at Lottie.

Lottie blinked twice. "I'm not sure how to respond to that. Oh, Jeeves," she called, signaling to their newly appointed butler. It took Brian a minute to respond to his butler name, so she waved at him. "Please put this in the kitchen."

In character, he did a small bow and strode off to the kitchen with the cake.

Lavinia pointed to a basket of shoes. "Make yourselves comfortable, and help yourself to slippers. You know we're a shoe-free house."

Doris huffed as she looked at the basket and, turning to me, said in a most indignant way, "I'd forgotten that the Labettes have a whole bunch of house rules. It's all very tiresome. No rules at my house. You just come in and sit down."

Gracie, however, looked as excited as a three-year-old. "Ooh, how wonderful! I'd forgotten how much I liked to play dress-up with my feet," she squealed, moving to sort through the basket.

Doris turned back to me and, in a clipped tone, said, "I have a pair in the car. I always keep my own set under the driver's seat, just in case you end up at one of these ridiculous shoe-free houses."

When she arrived back in the hallway, I was looking through the basket and Gracie was dancing around the hall with two completely different slippers on: one was made of red velvet and the other was an embroidered white slip on.

"I just can't decide," she said as she looked down at her feet. "I want to be a little devilish and scoot around in this red velvet one; but then this little white embroidered slipper reminds me of being a bride again. It seems more appropriate when we're at Flora's wedding shower to be wearing this little white one." She suddenly giggled. "Maybe I'll just wear one of each," she decided, making her way into the foyer.

As I pulled out a pair, Ruby arrived wearing a beautiful black silk beaded dress and a large white Marie Antoinette wig. Which was French, but this was Ruby, who always had to add her own twist. She had replaced her bangles and beads with a large fake pearl necklace and bracelet. She also had a beautifully embroidered fan, which she fanned herself with as she walked in.

The butler automatically introduced himself as Jeeves in a stern British way. Ruby smiled. "I love it," she said, batting him with her fan. "I think Flora is going to get a kick out of this."

I glanced around the paneled foyer. The sisters had already decorated for Christmas; the elegant crystal chandelier that dominated the center of their hall was strewn with fresh-cut holly and mistletoe.

Adorning their beautiful staircase, long gold-and-silver strings of beads hung from a fresh green pine garland, which was draped elegantly. It's piney fragrance mixed with the smell of fruity cocktails and the party food that Jeeves was now passing around on a tray.

From the main room, I could hear classical Mozart music playing, and I could smell even more exquisite aromas emanating from the kitchen.

The butler was suddenly by my side with a tray.

"Would madame like an hors d'oeuvre?" he said in a deep, booming voice.

"Yes, *madame* would," I joked back. I popped in a little shrimp puff pastry that melted in my mouth.

Just then, Flora arrived, just having been told ahead of time to arrive wearing something Edwardian. She was dressed in an incredible Edwardian outfit, her blonde hair piled up on top with a lovely Victorian clasp. She wore a delicate stole and an exquisite heart-shaped locket that her mother had given her.

Jeeves announced in a very grand tone, "The bride is here." Flora looked thrilled at the effort the sisters had made. She pulled a lovely pair of slippers out of her bag.

As we started to make our way into the main room, I noticed Ethel hovering in the corner of the hallway next to the Labettes' Christmas tree, which was impeccably dressed in designer crystal baubles and bows. She had been standing there like a scared rabbit since we arrived. As Doris moved toward the front room, she automatically shuffled behind. Lottie caught Ethel's arm.

"Ethel, honey, I wonder if you'd mind removing your shoes. We've had the floor rewaxed, and it's easy to scuff it right now. We have a basket of slippers over by the door. Why don't you help yourself to a pair?"

Ethel did not look impressed—her face communicated that loud and clear. I watched her rummage through the basket. Being barely five feet tall and a tiny woman, I guessed that her feet were no bigger than a five or six.

The basket was pretty picked over, with only the other red velvet slipper, the other white brocade slipper, a pair of slip-on socks, and some sheepskin moccasins left. She tried on the slipper socks first. They were very long and reached over her knees to her thighs. She looked like a miserable version of Pippi Longstocking. She shook her head and pulled them off. She reluctantly put on the sheepskin moccasins that appeared to be a couple of sizes too big. She looked like a grizzly bear. They were so large, she could hardly walk in them. So she just scooted across the floor.

When we moved into the main room, it almost took my breath away. The Labette sisters sure knew how to throw a party. The whole room was transformed by vases of white flowers, dozens of white candles, and classical music.

"Welcome to your Jane Austen bridal shower," Lottie announced. "We have a few fun gifts and a game to play."

She handed everybody a quill and a piece of parchment.

"First, the game," she said. "We are going to reenact some famous parts from Jane Austen's books, and you have to guess which books they're from."

Lottie and Lavinia proceeded to act out some of the most famous scenes from Jane Austen stories to the raucous laughter of the entire room. Well, nearly the entire room. Both Doris and Ethel seemed very confused about what was going on.

"*Sense and Sensibility*," shouted Ruby-Skye after one especially wonderful proposal from Lottie to Lavinia. She jumped to her feet without writing it down, and we all clapped.

"Why, if I'd had a man propose to me like that," said Lavinia, tapping her twin's cheek, "maybe I would have stayed married."

After we had finished the game, Flora opened our gifts: some beautiful candlesticks from Annie, a gorgeous Indian silk scarf from Ruby, and a gift card from Ethel. I had brought her some lovely Jane Austen leatherback books that I found in a second-hand shop, which she hugged to her chest with delight. And Lavinia and Lottie had bought her some quite sensational under-wear, a lilac lace camisole, and panties. We all roared with laughter when she pulled the lacy panties out of the box—everyone except Ethel, who just stared at it, her mouth agape.

The butler turned up and served us tea, and Doris made an announcement.

"I decided on a musical gift," she said dryly as she pulled out her bongo drums and handed a battered-looking maraca to

Ethel. She then started to tap out a rather ragged version of "Yellow Bird" as she hummed along, and Ethel shook the maraca with the least amount of enthusiasm she could summon. We all sat there, not quite sure how to respond.

The butler continued to hand out tea, and I could tell he was trying not to laugh as he offered a cup to Doris. "Would madame like a cup of tea after she has played with her bongos?" he asked solemnly.

Doris gazed at him, her eyes fixed as she concentrated. "Two sugars," she said in between verses as she continued to hum, and he obliged—but I was pretty sure he was sniggering—and left her cup on the side table with a slice of Doris's own walnut cake.

After the "performance," the Labettes announced they had a surprise. "I think you're going to love it," said Lottie. "I believe it's going to be perfect for your special day."

Flora's face registered slight irritation, as, I knew, she was getting more than fed up with the amount of "helpful" suggestions about her wedding.

Lavinia and Lottie stood on either side of the light blue silk drapes in front of their large picture window. Lavinia launched into a speech that sounded as if she'd been practicing all day. "Flora, darling, you are so dear to the both of us, almost like a daughter—if either of us had ever gotten around to having one."

There was a collective nod from the group.

"As we didn't, we felt the need to help you in any way that we could, especially during this most momentous occasion of your marriage, but we felt that one thing wasn't quite right. There is one thing we know that you've planned that we were hoping we could change your mind about. I know this is quite a big thing, so we don't want to rush you, but we think this will turn out for the best in the long run."

I glanced across at Flora. Her face frowned in anticipation of a surprise I wasn't sure she wanted.

"Outside of this window," said Lottie, stretching her arm

toward the curtains, "is something very extraordinary. Something I think you'll agree is going to make your wedding perfect."

Lottie nodded to Lavinia. Lavinia pulled hard on the braided gold tassel in one zealous sweeping gesture. Both the twins sang out in unison, "Ta-da!"

Standing at the window and leering in was a man with a smiling face. We all screamed, jumped to our feet, and dropped our cakes and cups in the process. All that could be heard was the sound of smashing china and spilling tea. Then, above it all, came one desperate voice: "Surely you're not expecting me to change my groom."

Lottie and Lavinia, taken aback by the reaction, glanced out of the window and screamed in unison, too.

"Oh my!" said Lottie. "Who is that?"

"Why, it's a man," said Lavinia as he waved at her. "I believe it's one of our landscapers."

"Wow," exclaimed Gracie, her eyes all aglow. "Her very own Mr. Darcy." Then, looking down at her sparkly silver wand, she added, "I had no idea this was so powerful." She then swished it around her head a couple of times and giggled.

"Oh, honey," said Lottie, moving quickly to Flora's side, who was shaking. "We love Dan. We wouldn't expect you to make that kind of a change. We just wanted to show you a little gazebo room that we think would convert into a lovely chapel for you, maybe for the evening affair, too. It has nothing to do with that man. I don't even know what he's doing there."

With the screams, the butler arrived at the door and slipped back into his American accent. "Is everybody OK?"

"There's a man," said Ethel, pointing a crooked finger toward the window in horror.

"A rather cute one," added Annie, laughing.

"Please deal with him, Jeeves," commanded Lottie.

"At once, madame," he said, returning to his British butler voice, and with a neat bow, he swept out of the room.

Lavinia worked to calm her hysterical sister, who was over-come with everything. The rest of us were on our hands and knees, clearing up broken china, when I heard Doris grumble to me as she tried to dab tea from the twins' Persian rug with soda, "Surprises are never good. There's no plate smashing or leering men at one of my rejection group meetings. This is what happens when we let our standards drop."

As Annie swept up cake crumbs, she added, "I've never been to a wedding shower where a young man was a wedding present. That's very novel."

A few minutes later, Jeeves issued in the young man, who looked very sheepish.

"Sorry if I startled you ladies," he said. "Just happened to leave my hat here in the garden when I was pruning Lavinia's tree."

I looked at his face. He looked down, avoiding my gaze, and I wasn't sure if he was telling the whole truth. I know the sisters had the gates unlocked to let us all in, but why hadn't he come directly to the door? Had he been listening at the window?

"This is John," said Lavinia with a wave of a hand. "He's one of our new landscapers."

"My goodness, you did give us a turn," said Lottie. "For a minute I thought my crazy sister had ordered a male stripper."

With that, Ethel sank into a chair. I thought she was going to pass out.

Soon the china disaster was cleared, and John stayed for a while. I noticed he was very interested in everything Flora had to say before eventually leaving. After he was gone, we took a tour of Lavinia and Lottie's little chapel, which was obviously in need of some refurbishment but was absolutely enchanting, with a beautiful view of the water through the windows. As we moved inside, they told us that it had once been used as a large game room for their poppa.

"It has seen lots of poker parties and rotary club meetings," Lottie informed us.

It was a spacious rectangular building with a beautiful vaulted ceiling and picture-box windows running down each side. Tables were stacked against one wall along with various pieces of exercise equipment and bicycles, plus a full-size snooker table, Ping-Pong table, and dartboard. At the bottom of the room, a huge arched window looked out onto the rolling waves of the Sound.

"Imagine everything emptied out and a lick of bright white paint on the walls," Lottie continued, becoming animated. "And rows of little wooden chairs on either side of a flower-strewn aisle. At the far end, on one side of the arched window, a magnificent blue spruce decorated with lights and bows in Flora's wedding colors. Down the aisle and in every window, pink and white poinsettias. Why, in fact," she linked arms with her sister, "you and Dan could walk right down the middle of the room right here." Lottie started to hum the "Wedding March" as she moved down the center of the room with Lavinia at her side.

"Don't get me going on that," remarked her twin. "You know that only brings back bad memories for me. I've marched down enough aisles in my time."

As we creaked along the cedar floor, we started to see the space through Lottie's eyes.

"We've had over one hundred and fifty people in here before now. We could do something with the windows; maybe add some fabulous silk drapes. And the view is spectacular."

We reached the end of the room, stepped up toward the window, first taking in the view of the water, then turning to regard the room from the opposite vantage point.

"Imagine getting married right in front of this window," I said wistfully.

"Exactly," said Lottie.

"I think it's a great idea," added Lavinia.

"You think I had a great idea?" said Lottie, putting her hand to her face in shock. "Will wonders never cease?"

The twins giggled.

"I would love to have it here," said Flora, her eyes wide with the anticipation. "I had planned to have it at the hotel in town, but after that awful fire, the community hall was all that was available. This, however, would be adorable." She twirled around in the space.

"We're so pleased," the twins exclaimed in unison.

"I love it," Flora added, beaming. "I can't wait to tell Dan."

We followed the sisters back through the room toward the door.

"We'll get a paint team in," Lottie confirmed over her shoulder. "And we'll bring extra chairs down from the attic and from the barn, get them all cleaned up."

We all stood in the driveway.

"It appears we've had enough excitement for one night," I said with a smile. "We should probably be going." It was getting on toward nine o'clock, and I needed to get home. I offered Flora a lift, but she shook her head. I knew she always liked to walk home, even in the dark. It was only a ten-minute walk to town from here. I watched her leave and smiled to myself. She was going to make a beautiful bride.

~

FLORA WALKED OUT OF THE TWINS' house and passed John's car. She noted he had out-of-state plates. When he saw her, he nodded from the driver's seat, and for a minute she thought he might be smoking. As Flora passed the car, he opened the window of his Pinto and asked her if she'd like a lift. Flora shook her head and informed him that she enjoyed walking into town and wanted to get some fresh air. She started to walk at a clip. Something about this young man unnerved her a little but she couldn't quite put her finger on what that might be.

The evening air was cold and sweet as she turned the corner onto Main Street and started down the Main Street hill. She took in a deep breath inhaling the salty air of the water and thought of Dan. She found that she felt a little sad. Of course she loved Dan and wanted to marry him, but all this fuss about the wedding was bothering her, and she felt tired. Usually a private person, it was disconcerting having strangers stop her in the street and tell her that she may want to wear a pale-pink lipstick or make sure to wear heels to float more elegantly down the aisle. Working in the flower shop didn't help one bit. Her employer, Mrs. Bickerstaff, was using her as some sort of advertising campaign. She would tell customers choosing a bouquet for a friend or a wife, "Why don't you try the dark-purple tulips? Flora's considering going in that direction for her wedding." Of course, she wasn't, but it seemed to work great for Mrs. Bickerstaff. Not only would they buy the tulips, but they would then launch into their own ideas of what they thought Flora should do with them. It was really starting to wear her down.

She sighed as she crossed Main Street and made her way up toward her cottage on the other side of town. She shuddered, a little uneasy. She felt as if someone was watching her. She looked around quickly but couldn't see anything out of place. She wasn't usually jumpy . . . it was probably all the wedding details getting her down. She pulled her wrap a little closer around her as her cottage came into view. It was a bright clear evening the night sky scattered with a thousand stars overhead and was usually her favorite time of day. There were just a few people in the street walking their dogs or heading to the pub at the end of the town.

She picked up her pace and reached into her bag for her key. She was glad to get through her little wrought iron gate and put the key in the lock. There it was again: that feeling that she was being watched. She placed the key quickly in the door and opened it.

Instantly her cat, Mr. Darcy, entwined himself around her legs. She reached down to pick him up and froze. Somewhere in the house, something had dropped to the ground. She held Mr.

Darcy close. Suddenly, the door to the kitchen flew open and there, standing in the doorway, was Dan. She let out the breath she had been holding.

He beamed at her. "Busted."

She dropped Mr. Darcy to the floor and flung herself into Dan's arms. She hadn't realized how much she'd needed him.

He responded jovially. "I hope you don't hug all of your burglars."

"Oh, I do," Flora whispered into his neck. "I find it a very effective tool for disarming them. I'm just so glad I'm marrying you and not some landscaper that the Labettes have lined up."

He loosened her grip so he could look into her face, a curious expression on his own. "Did I miss something?"

She answered him with a warm, soft kiss that expressed her deepest feelings. He wrapped his arms around her and drew her in for a gentle hug.

"Are you OK?" he asked as he rocked her gently in his arms. Having dated for two years, she knew he could sense when something was wrong.

"Mm-hmm," she murmured in a tone that seemed to convince him his first instinct had been right.

He pulled her back and looked deeply into her eyes. "No, you're not. Why don't you let me put the kettle on? You can tell me what going on."

She nodded. It was pointless to lie to him. Besides, she needed someone to talk to other than Mr. Darcy. As she retreated to the couch to take off her shoes and he to the kitchen, she shouted back toward him, "Then you can tell me why you're creeping around my kitchen this evening."

"Oh," he said, poking his head out of the kitchen door and smiling. "Well, that would have something to do with this." He appeared back in the living room with a vase of her favorite flowers: white lilies.

She melted. "Where did you get these?" she inquired, having a pretty good idea.

He laughed. "At the only flower shop in town," he smiled, handing them to her.

As he headed back into the kitchen, she inhaled their fragrant scent and smiled at his poor arrangement of them. "How did you get them out the shop without me knowing?"

"That was the hard part, but fortunately, I'm having a wild, passionate affair with a woman that works there, Mrs. Bickerstaff," he joked. "And she lets me sneak out flowers whenever I need to."

She smiled. She'd just remembered it was Thursday and that the flower shop stayed open late on Thursdays, but Flora had left early for her bridal shower.

"So I take it this is why you are here and I don't need to count the silver?"

He came back into the room and joined her on the sofa. He had made a pot of her favorite peppermint tea and poured her a cup.

"If you had any silver, then it's long gone by now. That's the real reason I'm marrying you, by the way."

She smiled as she took a sip of her tea and snuggled up, catlike, next to him. It was true. She had some inheritance after losing both her parents. As the only child, everything had gone to her.

"Seriously," he said. "What's wrong? I can tell you're unhappy." He laced his hand in hers, and she sighed.

"It's the wedding," she said without hesitation.

He pulled back, appearing taken off balance. "Don't tell me you're having second thoughts?" The concern on his face was real.

"No," she responded, squeezing his hand and snuggling deep into his shoulder.

"*Phew*," he responded, obviously relieved. "I'm glad, because I already bought my dress."

She laughed then and punched him playfully on the arm.

"What about the wedding?" he asked.

"When you proposed to me, I had this fairy-tale notion about how it would be. After my mom passed away, I thought that the planning would have been the hardest part of it, yet everybody and their aunt has been more than willing to share their opinion, and it's driving me mad. Everyone wants to tell me what color my flowers should be, the best bridesmaid dresses, caterers to hire, et cetera, et cetera. I haven't been left alone for a second to even think about what *I* really want. I just need some time to catch my breath."

"I know what you mean. It's the same at the garage. Everyone wants to know what color socks and tie I'm wearing," he said playfully.

She giggled. "You don't know how lucky you are. Nobody cares much about the groom, as long as he shows up."

"Well, I won't take that personally," he said. "I happen to think it's also pretty important that the bride shows up, too." He cuddled her then.

"You know what I mean," she responded. "I just wish we could run away. At this time of year when I was young, Mom and Dad would take me to a little bed and breakfast in Leavenworth. It was called the Nest, tucked up high in the mountains. I would walk for miles in the snow or enjoy the little wood-burning fireplace in our bedroom, drinking hot chocolate snuggled under blankets. I would take a book and curl up there all day and watch the snow as the wind would take hold of it, blowing it into flurries, making it sway and dance and then fall into drifts. I would close my eyes and listen to the wood crackle and pop in the fireplace. I'd spend blissful afternoons falling asleep that way, with the smell of chocolate and cinnamon infiltrating my dreams."

Dan smiled at her and pulled her closer.

"This is how I became a poet. I would listen to the wind and the fire, and the intoxicating experience started to roll across my mind, becoming words. I know it sounds silly now, but I never felt safer than when I was sleeping in front of those little fires. In fact, when Dad passed away, it was the only place I wanted to go to after the funeral. Mom wasn't up to it, so I caught the train all the way there and spent a week at the Nest. It was also the place I went to when Mom passed away after Dad, four years ago." Flora's voice trailed away.

Dan appeared to feel the pain that filled the room. He took her hand. "I know you wish your mom were here," he said quietly as he drew her in closely again.

Flora hadn't really been feeling sad, but suddenly, from nowhere, silent tears started to slide down her face. "I hadn't realized that until right now," she said, surprised by her emotion. She pulled a cotton handkerchief from her pocket and blew her nose. "Everyone has been giving me their opinion, but deep down it was just my mom's voice I wanted to hear."

He held her tightly, kissing her gently.

She cried quietly for a while; then she blew her nose and felt much better. She hadn't even realized that her mother's passing was bothering her, but now it seemed obvious as she felt the void.

"Maybe I can help with your plans," he said gently.

She smiled. He was being kind, but she knew he wouldn't be of any help for what she needed. "Good," she said coyly. "Tomorrow you can help me pick out the right shade of pink for my roses."

He blinked "There's more than one shade of pink?" he responded with mock horror.

She shook her head, thinking about how everything felt just right with the world when she was lying in his arms.

CHAPTER SIX

POOPY & DRIBBLE: THE SEQUEL

The next morning, we stood at SeaTac baggage claim at eleven a.m., waiting for the arrival of the grandbabies. We had both been down to San Francisco many times to stay with Stacy and Chris, and we had just seen them at Thanksgiving. But this was the first time we were going to have them with us for an extended amount of time. Martin had said she'd been vague when he'd asked how long she'd be staying and implied it was longer than just a weekend break. I knew Stacy and Chris had had their ups and downs over the last eighteen months, adjusting to this pair of energy bugs, but I hoped that my suspicions weren't realized and that the marital stress I had been seeing was not causing them to drift apart.

I eagerly watched the crowd roll out of the gates—mainly business travelers pulling little suitcases on wheels as they rushed to appointments and jobs. And as I scanned the arrival board, I noticed that Stacy's plane had landed nearly forty-five minutes ago. What could be taking them so long?

Martin stood by my side. He had taken the morning off to pick up Stacy and was whistling to himself as he waited. I couldn't contain my worry.

"I hope they're all right and that the babies have not been affected too much by the flight." I barely finished my sentence when I heard it: a sound like the faint hum of an incoming insect. But as it grew closer, the sound crescendoed into what was unmistakably the wail of two young babies crying at the top of their lungs.

Martin stopped whistling and smiled wryly. "They sound fine to me," he said, upbeat. "And they could have a career as a human typhoon warning system, for sure."

As the sound of the crying reached a fever pitch, I spotted them. James was slung over on his mother's hip, his little hands balled up as he punched wildly at Stacy's shoulder. His face was red and angry, and his tiny mouth screeched the word *"No"* over and over. In the stroller, Livvy, in pink tights and hair in bunches with bows, was kicking her legs wildly in the air. Her face was angry and blotchy from crying.

Stacy had a diaper bag slung over her free shoulder, and two other bags hung on the handle of the stroller. A binky was pinned to the front of her creased shirt, her hair was in some kind of mangled bun and she was wearing sweatpants. I marveled at what motherhood had done to her. My pristine, had-it-all-together, type A–character daughter was baby mush. It had brought out the best and the worst in her.

As Stacy spotted us, she said to the kids, "Oh look, there's Grammy and Grandpa," which in turn only seemed to escalate the screams to shrieks.

"Looks like they've arrived," Martin murmured to me. "And don't they take after their mother."

I reprimanded him by tapping him on the arm and girded myself with a smile. I raced to meet them as they passed through security into the main part of the airport.

Stacy thrust a bucking James into my arms, which only infuriated him more as he started to take his frustration out on me by bending as far out of my arms as he could in a full backbend. His mouth widened in a crimson-faced howl. Martin reached forward and kissed Stacy on the cheek, saying, "Sounds like you've had a lovely flight."

Stacy rolled her eyes. "You have no idea how bad it was." She filled us in on all the things the twins had managed to do on the plane, finishing up with, "And they haven't stopped screaming from the minute I left San Francisco until the moment we got off here."

Grabbing two bags from Stacy and picking up Livvy, Martin said, "Let's get your luggage. Your baggage claim is over here."

Making our way to the conveyor belt, there seemed to be no one left waiting from Stacy's flight, yet the conveyor belt seemed full. Slowly, Martin and I realized that the traveling circus of increments on the belt all belonged to Stacy: two car seats, four suitcases, two play saucers, and another stroller. Martin and I stood with our mouths open in disbelief.

He whispered to me, "What, no kitchen sink? I'm definitely going to be spending a lot of time in my workshop."

I nudged him and snapped back, "Over my dead body."

It took two carts and all of us to haul everything to the car.

"How could two tiny people need so much?" Martin whispered again as he started to pack and shove boxes into the trunk. "I only remember having a stroller when Stacy was young."

"Oh, it's a whole new world," I said. As we slammed the trunk shut, even with all the doors closed, we could still hear the twins protesting while Stacy strapped them into their car seats.

My daughter suddenly shouted, "Livvy just threw up on your coat, Mom, I'm so sorry."

Martin smirked at me. "Glad I'm still wearing mine. We could run now. We're right at the airport. Let's take a plane to Hawaii, let them figure it out for themselves."

I was actually tempted.

As we made our way into the screaming metal box and started

the car, Stacy handed me a CD over my shoulder. "Play this," she said. "it will help."

I put the CD into the player as Martin made his way out of the airport parking lot. It was hard to hear anything above the noise—and now there was kicking into the back of my seat. James had apparently decided this was the best way to get Grandma's attention.

Martin pumped up the music on the CD player as "Old MacDonald Had a Farm" blared out. The song was just getting to the loud pig noises "on the farm" when Martin wound down the window to pay for parking. The young man taking the tickets looked taken aback by the sheer volume of screaming and music. "Got yourself a regular show going on there," he commented.

Martin quipped back, "I have no idea what you're talking about. I went deaf about five minutes ago."

"They're tired," yelled Stacy as we left the airport and entered the freeway. "Give them about twenty minutes and they'll both be asleep."

Martin looked at me with disbelief, but sure enough, within a short distance, both the twins were sleeping soundly.

"I had them up so early this morning," she said as she ran a hand through her wild hair and stared zombielike out the window. She sounded exhausted. I tried to decide if I was going to broach the elephant in the room—or the lack thereof.

It appeared that Martin had the same thought. "Chris decided not to come with you, then?" he asked quietly.

The awkward silence that followed confirmed our fears. I turned and saw the tears streaming down her face, and I knew. I reached between the seats and held my daughter's hand. I'd suspected things were strained ever since we had been down to see them, but now I could see it clearly on her face. Things were not going well at all.

CHAPTER SEVEN

DUSTY OLD WEDDING DRESSES &
FLEMISH NUNS

The next morning, I finally found the ringing phone that one of the twins had tucked into the cutlery drawer. I followed its muffled sound around the kitchen for five rings until I located it just before voice mail clicked in. It was Flora, and something was wrong with her tone.

"Are you busy today?" she asked. "I could use some support."

"Let me see what Stacy has planned, and I will call you back," I said. I hung up and turned from the kitchen counter just in time to catch Livvy as she was trying to launch herself into the trash can. I picked her up and walked upstairs. As Stacy had only just arrived, the last thing I wanted to do was leave her on her own. Our relationship had been rocky over the years, and I was hoping for some quality time with her while she was with me.

I caught up with her as she was heading out of the shower, her hair wrapped in a towel turban.

"Did I hear the phone?" she asked.

"Yes, it was Flora."

Stacy leaned forward and rubbed her hair, drying off the ends. "How are the wedding plans going?" she asked as she flicked her dampened hair back onto her shoulders.

"Things aren't going exactly to plan." I paused before emphasizing the words, *"Doris Newberry!"*

Stacy smiled knowingly, having had her own encounters with Doris in the past.

"She was hoping that I might be able to join her for a fitting today, but I told her that you were here and I thought we would probably want to spend time together."

Stacy looked uncomfortable. "Actually, it's OK, Mom," she said," I have a friend coming over in a little while to keep me company."

I tried not to show the pain I was feeling from a stab in my heart. "Oh," I exclaimed, taking in a sharp breath. *"Friend,"* I said, my voice a little tight, knowing full well that Stacy had no friends that I knew of on the island.

"Annie's coming over," said Stacy, walking back into the bathroom to brush her hair. I felt a sharp jab again. So when she'd said her *friend*, she meant one of my friends.

"We're going to watch soaps together," she added as she pulled a hairdryer out of the drawer. I continued to feel the tightness in my chest.

I was glad that she and Annie had bonded, but it always felt a little sad that Stacy and I weren't as close as I'd always wanted us to be. I had hoped that now the babies were here, maybe we'd have some time to get to know each other and get closer.

"No problem," I said airily as I tried to push down the hurt feelings that had now taken hold of my throat, "I'll go hang out with Flora, then."

"Wonderful!" said Stacy, obviously glad to finish the conversation.

I stepped over the top of the stairway gate and made my way down the stairs just as there was a knock at the door. I opened it —it was Annie. I tried not to show my disappointment. I really was glad that Stacy had found a friend.

"Hi, Annie," I said, my voice sounding a little more jubilant than normal.

She came inside. In her arms were bundles of new clothes for the twins, and she'd also knitted two little teddy bears: one in pink and one in blue.

"Where are my adopted nephew and niece?" she said in a jovial tone.

"Annie!" shouted Livvy in her sweet little voice.

"I didn't realize the twins knew you that well," I responded, shocked to hear Livvy call out to her like that.

"Oh, we talk on the phone all the time," chuckled Annie, shutting the front door.

Stacy came downstairs with the twins—who had both been tugging on the stairway gate—and smiled at her friend.

"I have treats!" said Annie, her eyes glowing. "We are going to see if Richard's baby is really his," she said, apparently making some reference to the program they both like to watch.

As Stacy nodded, I turned to my daughter. "I didn't know you like soaps so much."

She looked exasperated and let out a huge sigh. "There's not much to do at home in the morning with the twins, so I have become quite addicted," she said, smiling at Annie. "Annie and I keep up on all of them," she informed me. "She even sends me the soap magazines."

"Soap magazines?" I exclaimed. I had no idea there was such a thing.

As the twins pattered excitedly behind Annie, they all made their way into the front room, and I made my way out the front door. As I walked down the path toward the car, I couldn't help wondering to myself, *Why don't I like to knit or watch soaps?* I have to admit that I was just a little jealous. I got into the car and called Flora—she needed me. I told her I was on my way, then I headed down my driveway and into town.

Ten minutes later, I picked up Flora and we arrived at Charlotte's dress shop in town, which also had a small supply of wedding dresses. Flora waited outside the door patiently as I parked the car. There were only two shops together here on Third Street—the *high end of town*, as it was called since it was away from the hustle and bustle of the rest of the village. The other shop was a little kitchen supply store that provided the inhabitants of Southlea Bay with every type of kitchen accoutrement.

I rang the bell; Charlotte's, being so exclusive, was always locked. Her bleak white face appeared in the doorway. As always, I thought it was odd that the shop owner was called *Charlotte*. The name didn't seem to fit her character at all. She had grown up in France with a very Bohemian lifestyle and apparently was related to a duke or a lord in England. She was an elegant thin woman with straight black hair and chalk-white skin. She always wore the latest designer glasses and thick black eyeliner. She was sophisticated, but she had an air about her that seemed to indicate everything bored her, including her customers.

She was wearing thick black tights and a wool skirt. The bottom of the skirt ballooned out, and threads of a variety of colors dangled along the edges, maypolelike. She looked like a black jellyfish with wildly colored tentacles. I couldn't help thinking as I watched Charlotte unlock the door that Stacy's twins would love pulling on that skirt.

As she pulled the door open, her skirt swished from side to side like a bell. She also wore a starched white shirt with oversize, pointed lapels and black-and-white patent leather shoes. A thick black rope of hair hung in front of her right shoulder, and on her chest was a line of carefully placed safety pins. But the piece de resistance was what she wore on her head: a stark bonnet that could have come straight out of a sixteenth-century Flemish painting hanging in an art gallery . She looked odd, but stylish—like a modern-day nun.

She forced a stiff smile of acknowledgment at Flora, which

barely made it onto her lips before it was gone. As we came in, she didn't say anything, just kind of jerked her head to tell us to move forward.

We did as we were told, and Charlotte locked the door firmly behind us.

"This way," she said curtly in her thick French accent.

Yes, I thought as I followed her slow pace through the shop, *her name should be Yvonne or Clarice.* The name *Charlotte* made me think of a playmate for Anne of Green Gables, a fresh-faced child with apple cheeks, layered dresses, and a straw bonnet. It definitely didn't fit this aloof swan with Parisian style and strait-laced headgear.

I looked at Flora, who was following behind. She looked terri-fied by the whole experience, so I grabbed her hand and smiled. It was cold and limp. She smiled back weakly, unsure.

"It's going to be great," I said.

Charlotte showed us into the fitting room and introduced us to Carrie, whom I believed was her niece, even though she always called her employer *Ms. Charlotte.* She was dressed like a muddled mini version of her boss, but she was bigger boned and round, so the outfit didn't hang in quite the same way as it would have on gaunt figures walking down a European catwalk. She looked as if she would have been more comfortable in a pair of jeans and fleece. Carrie followed Flora into a curtained fitting room.

I looked around the racks while I waited. Charlotte posi-tioned herself back at her desk, where she started wrapping clothes. She asked in a thick accent, "Would you care for some fruit tea?"

I smiled. "No, thank you."

She looked visibly relieved, as if that would be the end of her small talk, and headed to a rack of clothes that she arranged neatly into shiny white boxes with the word *Charlotte's* scrawled on the front in black loop letters. She then filled the boxes with black-and-white tissue paper. I was looking about when my eyes caught new customers: the Labette twins were at the door, grinning at me.

Charlotte stiffly made her way to open the door, trying a brighter tone that seemed to be a great effort. "Come in, come in."

Lavinia walked in and seemed unaffected by Charlotte's sullen presence or the fact the somber air of the store would have made an undertaker proud.

"*Darrrrling*," Lavinia said, rolling her words in her usual way. "Fancy seeing you here."

I smiled. "What a lovely surprise. Are you looking for anything special?"

Lavinia nodded "We are on the hunt for just the right hat for Flora's wedding. We had what we thought we were going to wear but . . ."

"I liked it a lot," Lottie piped up. "Black never goes out of style, now, does it, Charlotte?"

"I am just the shop owner." Charlotte shrugged, appearing not to know or care.

Lavinia picked up the thought. "Honey, I agree, it is a lovely hat, but the last time we wore it was for Poppa's funeral. It doesn't seem appropriate to wear a funeral hat if we are bridesmaids at a wedding."

Flora slipped out from behind the curtain of the fitting room and onto a platform in the center with a three-way mirror. We all gasped in unity.

"Well, Flora, darling," gushed Lavinia. "I don't think I've ever seen you look so lovely. You are truly beautiful."

I looked at Flora, who had allowed just a little glow to creep to her cheeks. She looked enchanting, as if she'd just walked out of a vintage Victorian magazine. The dress was a mixture of satin and antique lace, in off white. It was gathered at her tiny waist with a satin bow studded with exquisite pearls. The sweetheart neckline highlighted her delicate bone structure perfectly, and the sleeves of transparent lace that showed just a hint of skin were fastened at the wrist by small mother-of-pearl buttons. The same buttons lay in a long elegant line down her back.

We all gathered around her as Carrie, with a bouquet of pins in her mouth, added a couple to the side of the dress. Charlotte swished from her station, bell-like, toward the dress with a critical eye. "Turn around for me," she said. She sighed deeply as she noticed the pins in the sides of the dress. "Flora, please do not lose any more weight. You will knock out the balance and the style."

Flora flushed. "I'm not trying to lose any weight," she said softly. "It just seems to keep falling off me."

"You must eat more," rebuked Charlotte, studying the skirt a little more carefully. She said something to her niece in French, who then bustled off to fetch something from the back room. All three of us stood there, gushing and cooing.

All of a sudden, there was a hard rap on the window of the shop. I looked across, and there, staring in the window, were Ethel and Doris. In Doris's hand was a newly wrapped wooden spoon with a bow. Charlotte seemed alarmed at being summoned to the door in such a way, and she appeared to swear under her breath in French. In her native tongue, it seemed so much more emphatic. She walked to the door and unlocked it but stood in the doorway.

"Can I help you?" she said in a tone that was as frosty as Jack himself.

Doris didn't seem the least bit intimidated by this black stick insect with the swinging bell skirt and a wimple. "I'm with them," she said, pointing at the three of us with her wooden spoon. She then added, with emphasis, "I'm Flora's *wedding coordinator*."

Lavinia took over with her own pleasantries. "Darling Doris, come on in. We're having a regular party. It's Flora's dress fitting."

Doris bustled in with Ethel following closely behind, leaving Charlotte no choice but to step aside or be knocked down as

Doris plowed straight toward the mirrors. She instantly took over, studied the dress Flora was wearing, and said, "What are your other choices? I mean, you're going to get married in white, aren't you?"

Flora blinked, caught completely off guard.

"Why, this *is* white," I said, tapping Flora's hand, who looked like she had been shocked dumb.

"Really?" said Doris, peering at the lace. "Then this lace needs a good wash. Maybe it's been hanging in the back of the shop for who knows how long. You never see a soul in here, so it could've been here for years."

Not to be upstaged, Charlotte swept over and took control. "The lace is Austrian with a hint of cream, and very exclusive. The princess of Denmark had it sewn into her wedding gown. To whom am I speaking?" she asked, sharply.

Not looking up from scrutinizing the dress she said, "you can call me *Doris* or *Mrs. Newberry.*"

"I am Charlotte," she said as she straightened to confront the ballsy woman who had just taken over her shop. Her tone reflected her disgust over the fact that Doris had not even given her the common decency to properly introduce herself.

"So this is your place," said Doris with a sniff as she glanced around, unimpressed. "I've always wondered who it belonged to —anytime I'm here buying my kitchen equipment." She lifted the wooden spoon as if to emphasize what she'd been doing. "I wouldn't think you were the owner, as you are dressed"—she looked down at Charlotte's outfit—"like a shop assistant."

She then caught a sight of one of Charlotte's dangly threads and couldn't help herself. She leaned forward and snapped it off before any of us could stop her. Charlotte opened her mouth in horror, but nothing came out. Doris just smiled and held up the thread. "You had a loose thread," she said.

Charlotte rushed from the room and started issuing French instructions in a stern tone to Carrie, who was wide-eyed and just as shocked but automatically started following her boss's orders. She raced into an adjoining room and returned with two gilded gold chairs with black-and-white ticking. She placed them down in the center of the shop, and Charlotte barked at Doris, "You will sit."

Doris seemed to miss the harsh tone and said, "Thank you." She and Ethel settled themselves down as Doris shouted at the assistant, "I would love a cup of coffee."

Charlotte and Carrie continued to pin, mumbling in French as they moved around Flora, who was now looking down at the color with apparent regret. I read her thoughts, stepped behind her, and looked at her in the mirror, reassuring her she looked perfect.

Doris settled herself, taking out her phone to make a call, and Ethel pulled out a bag of sweets and started sucking something to death. They continued to watch Flora as if it were a picnic at the zoo.

Lavinia started moving about the shop, trying on hats. She continued to chat with Charlotte, totally oblivious to the monotone one-word answers she received in return.

"What about this one?" she asked. She'd picked up a bright-red hat with a broad brim that would have looked fabulous on Audrey Hepburn. Grabbing a leopard-patterned jacket from the hanger, she slung it over her shoulder and paraded up and down the store, pretending she was a model on a catwalk. "I love red," she said as she continued. "I've always wanted to be a scarlet woman."

Lottie, who was looking at lace gloves in a wooden drawer, didn't look up when she said dryly, "What do you mean 'wanted to be'?"

Suddenly, the doorbell rang. Everyone looked toward the window. Ruby-Skye was peering in with her hands up to her eyes, trying to look inside.

Charlotte did not look amused by this outburst of odd old

ladies descending upon her store, which probably never had more than ten customers a month. She moved slowly to the door and didn't even ask Ruby who she was. She stood aside with distinct displeasure and bid her to come in.

Ruby was dressed in one of her own zany ensembles: a fire-red jumpsuit with gold trim, green sneakers, and hair woven into a yellow scarf. She had on her usual arm decorations, and huge looped earrings hung from her ears. As I watched the two conversing from the back of the shop, it seemed like some sort of odd, eclectic variety show, with Charlotte's bell-like swinging and nunlike nodding and Ruby's musical bangles clashing.

"You must be Charlotte," said Ruby-Skye, who appeared to be out of breath. She took Charlotte's hand and shook it powerfully, saying, "I've always wanted to meet you. I also have a store. I own the Wool Emporium down the street. We're both in the same trade. I've never managed to make it up to your clothes shop, though. I hear they're way too expensive."

Charlotte pulled her hand back from Ruby-Skye as if she were taking it from a bear trap and stared at her with obvious distaste. It was evident by her expression that she didn't want to be associated with anyone of this caliber. "I think we have very different customers," she said, swishing back toward her desk. "So I don't think there's any way we can compare ourselves to being in the same trade."

"Wait," said Ruby, stopping Charlotte in her tracks. I watched with horror as she also leaned forward and snagged another colorful thread from her skirt and handed it to Charlotte, saying, "Don't worry, I got it."

Charlotte snatched at it and marched the rest of the way to her desk.

"Why, this is turning into a regular party," said Lavinia, now adding red pumps to her ensemble. "Charlotte, do you have any music we could boogie to?"

Charlotte looked horrified at the prospect and said, "I have another fitting in twenty minutes."

Oblivious to Charlotte's cold inflection, Lavinia approached Ruby-Skye and kissed her on both cheeks. "How did you know we were all here?"

"I called," said Doris through a mouthful of Ethel's boiled sweets. "I asked her to come and check out Flora's dress."

Ruby-Skye nodded. "So I put a sign on the door, and I ran up here in about ten minutes flat." She then walked straight up to Flora and took out her glasses to study the dress. Flora looked as if she was beginning to feel like an animal in a cage.

"It does have some cream undertones," she said thoughtfully. Then she looked up at Flora. "But I think it brings out her complexion beautifully," she added, staring back again at the dress. "I believe it will do."

"Mon Dieu!" Charlotte said.

"The problem," said Doris, "is the light in this pokey shop."

Charlotte's eyes hit the ceiling, and she spluttered out a French swear word that she didn't even try to hide. Then she started to rant at her niece, who was red faced and flushed, pinning one of Flora's hems. Charlotte continued without even hiding the fact she was talking about Doris, made even more evident by pointing at her. Doris, on the other hand, seemed completely oblivious at Charlotte's growing frustration. She bounded out of the chair, stood next to Ruby-Skye, and took out her own glasses.

"Yes," she said decisively. "It's the lighting in this shop. It doesn't give you a clear idea of what the final color will be."

I could see Flora was close to tears, but before I could say anything to defend her, Doris said, "Step closer to the window, Flora."

Without giving Flora a chance to respond, Doris took her by the elbow and shuffled her toward the door of the shop. Flora obliged her because she didn't really have any choice, and Doris nearly bowled over Carrie, who was practically still attached to the gown.

"This is very exclusive," said Charlotte, moving alongside Doris with haste, as if she feared she would make off with her dress with Flora still in it.

"I just want to see it in the light," snapped Doris. "After all, this is Flora's big day. It might need a little scrub with some bleach water. I think this will be the time to find out."

"I think it looks adorable," Lottie piped up as she tried on an exquisite pair of gloves. "In fact, I believe we should all go in cream accessories to match the bride."

Charlotte bounded across the length of the shop and squared off with Doris, but Doris pushed her aside as if she were nothing more than a ragdoll. Before anyone could say anything, she opened the door and pulled Flora into the street. I ran to her side —Flora needed to be rescued, and she needed to be rescued now.

"That's better," said Doris as she appeared to reevaluate the color.

Suddenly, someone honked their horn, and we all looked around. There, waving at us from the car, was Dan, who had just been driving past. Flora shrieked and ran back in the shop, pulling Doris and Ruby with her, who both still had a firm hold of the dress on either side. She ran straight over Carrie, who had come to join them at the doorway and had just taken hold of the bottom of the dress to straighten a pin. Flora tripped over the top of her, and what followed was a long, tearing sound followed by echoing silence.

Flora detangled herself from Carrie and raced to the back of the store as she burst into tears. All the women froze except me. I made my way to the dressing room, where Flora had fallen into a large lace-and-satin heap in the center of the floor.

I knelt down beside the sobbing girl and said, "Flora, it's going to be OK. It's just the hem. I'm sure Charlotte will be able to fix it."

"It's not that," she said, forcibly wiping her tears with the heel of her hand. "Dan just drove by while we were standing outside, and he saw me. He saw me in my wedding dress. That's bad luck for him to see me before the wedding." She plunged into tears again, and I rooted a tissue out from my pocket and handed it to her.

"That is superstitious poppycock," I said. "There's no one more suited to be together than you and Dan, and you're going to have a very long and happy life together. You just wait and see."

CHAPTER EIGHT

A BUMP ON A LOG & REVEREND DORIS

John sat in the center of the circle of ladies, feeling as out of place as a pork chop at a Jewish wedding. He had arrived at Doris's ten minutes before, greeted by the short woman with the grumpy expression. Now he found himself seated in the middle of this odd-looking front room on a blue-and-white stripy deck chair, right in the center. He had looked around the room and already forgotten most of their names, and before he could say anything, a plate of what looked like coconut cake and a cup of tea had been thrust into his hand. He didn't get a chance to tell them he didn't really like tea or cake, so he just sat there holding them, with everyone all staring at him like a first grader at show-and-tell.

This was not what John had planned. He could feel all of his sharpened streetwise senses being sucked from him as the women wore him down, one sugary smile at a time.

He had never meant to be here: He had been waiting outside Flora's house to speak to her now that he knew where she lived. He had been smoking under a lamppost, waiting for her to come out so he could confront her with what he knew, when he was accosted by Lavinia Labette, who had been dropping something off at Flora's for the wedding. In trying to come up with a story, he'd said he was there to talk to Flora about their book club. The next thing he knew, Lavinia had said she was on her way to a meeting, that Flora was probably already there, and, looping her arm in his, had announced that he was welcome to come with her. Not finding a way to back down without lying again, he'd had to come along, hoping to pull Flora aside somehow.

"So," said Lavinia, pointing her cake fork in his direction, "tell us everything."

He stared back blankly.

Lottie must have sensed John's discomfort. "Oh, Lavinia, let the man drink his tea and eat his cake."

John took up his fork, happy to oblige. This would give him time to think. Who was he? Where was he from? What story was he going to tell them? He looked across at Flora, who was sipping her tea. How would he get her alone?

"I think John has a secret!" said Annie, giggling.

John swallowed hard. Had she read his mind?

"I think he has a *love of his life* he's not telling us about," Annie finished.

John sighed relief. "Nope," he said. "I'm all single."

"Well, that makes two of us," Lavinia said, squeezing his knee. "But maybe not for long."

John was horrified. Maybe coming here had been a bad idea. Flora sat all the way across the room from him, and with everyone seated in a circle like this, it would be hard to pull her aside without everyone knowing.

Doris suddenly arrived in the room and banged a big wooden gavel on the table.

He was taken aback. What was this? *The People's Court*?

"First, the pledge," said Doris.

John looked around the room for a flag and absently placed his hand across his heart. But instead of the Pledge of Allegiance, every woman took hands and recited some sort of poem about being rejected. He realized again why he hated small towns. None of this made any sense to him. Once they finished their pledge, two of the women eagerly announced that they had rejection letters, and Doris shouted, "Get the book!"

Off went the little grumpy one, and John watched as Annie, the crazy knitting lady in the corner, pulled out a letter, as did that hippie woman. She seemed to be wearing a purple bedsheet. Around her waist hung a thick metal chain that looked as if a dog should be attached to the other end, and on her head, a pink turban. *Maybe she's going to tell us our fortune,* he thought as he swallowed another lump of the cake he was barely tasting.

Yep, he hated small towns.

When the little grumpy one arrived back, she was carrying what appeared to be a massive photo album. Doris opened it and started to brag about all the rejection letters they had received from publishers. He sat in total disbelief as they began to read one rejection letter after another. Crazy. They were all completely crazy. Once she had finished, she took the new letters from the members, and a jar was passed around to collect money "for a local charity," he was told.

Doris banged her gavel down on the table again. "Now, it's time to read!"

"Oh, goody!" said Gracie. "I have a fairy story to share."

"I've got a horror," said Ruby.

"And I've brought some spice!" said Lavinia as she winked at John.

He shoved another spoonful of the cake into his mouth. While they all were getting excited about reading their books, he slipped the cup of tea, now cold, onto a side table, hoping that no one would notice. If only Flora would move into a different room. He would just ask if they could have coffee in town somewhere; then he would be able to confront her.

The pink turbaned lady stood up. "I shall start with my piece, 'Dead Bodies from Outer Space,'" she declared. "It is more of a performance art." In one hand, she held a scrappy bit of paper as she paraded around the room. She described a world where aliens used Earth as their cemetery. She contorted her body into odd positions and projected her voice dramatically. It wasn't very well written, but it was definitely compelling.

When she finished reading, the little old lady—Gracie, rose to her feet as if she were at a school assembly, with a neat piece of writing in her hand. She read a fairy story about toadstools and gnomes. Her eyes glistened as she informed John, "I generally write about growing up in England during World War II, but today I felt like writing a fairy story." She then nodded and sat down.

"Now," said Doris, bringing them all to order, "I have a surprise for you all. Ethel and I will be back in a minute, as I will need her to help me." John watched as they disappeared upstairs. He didn't really need any more surprises tonight.

Lavinia's eyes shone as she suddenly spoke, "John, I think you should escort me to Flora's wedding. You could be my plus one."

John looked across at Flora and felt a twinge of guilt—here they were, talking about her wedding when he was here to ruin it. Flora seemed like an OK person, and this was enough to give him second thoughts about his plans.

Flora looked down. "You're welcome to come with Lavinia if you wish," she said quietly, nibbling on her cake.

John didn't respond. He hoped to be long gone before Flora's wedding, if there was even going to be one. He stabbed at the last few mouthfuls of his food. He couldn't believe what he'd gotten himself into here. He felt stifled. He needed to think. None of this was turning out how he had expected, and as distant as he'd been, they actually seemed to like him. They acted as if they liked being around him. Since he had met them at the twins' house, they had gone out of their way to be nice to him whenever he ran into them in town. It had been a long time since he had felt that he hadn't had to earn his place in a group—a long time since he'd felt accepted just for being himself. Annie moved over and held her latest knitting project up in front of him.

"Nearly done," she said, her face lighting up. "I'm hoping to have it finished for you for Christmas. I just need to measure the length of the arms."

It wasn't until she produced a tape measure from her pocket and started calculating the length of his arm that he realized what she was saying: the sweater she was knitting was for him.

Why would she do that? She hardly knew him. As she nodded and made notes on a writing pad, it made him think of his grandma. She died when he was young, but she had always knitted things for him to wear. He actually felt a bit choked up. He swallowed his brimming emotion down hard. He had to get this thing with Flora over with, put a stop to all this new emotion. He didn't like how it made him feel. He jumped to his feet. He had to leave. He made a lame excuse and was gone.

∿

I WAS LATE GETTING to Doris's, as I had spent time helping Stacy get the twins ready for bed. I passed John in the driveway at a clip, barely acknowledging my *hello*. As he dashed toward the road, another vehicle pulled into the driveway.

"Ernie!" I exclaimed, making my way to the driver's side of his car. He rolled down the window with a broad smile, revealing a couple of his gold teeth. He'd always struck me as a dapper older gentleman but with a mischievous, childlike spirit. We had met Ernie in Medford, Oregon, when we were on our road trip. He had become a dear friend, who had also performed in our musical show the year before.

"What are you doing up here?" I asked.

"I was summoned by her majesty to come up for Flora's wedding. I guess I'm her guest!" he said in his deep, resonating tone.

I linked arms with him as we walked up to the door together.

But when Doris opened the front door, we were both taken aback. Instead of her regular clothes, she was dressed from head to toe in a huge tent like white cassock, a starched clerical collar, and around her neck, flowing vestments with embroidered gold crosses on either side.

Ernie chuckled. "I just met her I swear," he joked, unhooking his arm from mine. "I didn't realize this was a setup—or am I here for confession?" he inquired, his eyes wide. "Because the latter could take a while."

"Come in, come in," said Doris briskly. "I'm just about to make a big announcement."

Ernie and I looked at each other, shrugged, and made our way toward the front room.

She opened the door and pushed us in ahead of her so we could find a seat before she made her entrance. Behind us, she coughed to get everyone's attention.

They all turned and watched, wide-eyed and openmouthed, as she floated reverently into the center of the room.

"I have an incredible announcement for Flora," she said with great pomp and ceremony. "I am now ordained by the church. My final papers arrived the other day, so I can now officially marry you and Dan." An ostentatious smile spread across her face.

Flora looked horrified.

"So that's the secret you've been keeping," said Lavinia tartly. "That's why Mrs. Barber was galloping up and down Main Street the other week, isn't it?"

"That was a misunderstanding," said Doris briskly. "She saw the official church seal and thought I had a letter from the pope himself. Being a devout Catholic, she felt some urgency in communicating his eminence's wishes to me. But I cleared it up with her later and let her know I am actually just a humble

Universal minister, and I have nothing to do with that guy at the Vatican."

"I thought priests were men," commented Gracie wistfully.

"Not anymore." Lottie shook her head. "Now anyone can get ordained on the Internet."

"Which means," added Doris, "I can write your service, Flora, and help you with your vows."

"I've already asked Lavinia's pastor to lead the service," Flora said in a desperate tone.

But Doris would have none of it. "I already spoke to him, and he thought it would be a great idea, if that's what Flora wanted. I assured him it would be. Just think of all the fun we will have planning the service now!" Doris's eyes sparkled.

"Right," Flora answered quietly. She didn't seem convinced.

"Now," said Doris, "I have another surprise."

"I'm not sure my heart can take it," Lottie whispered to me as she rolled her eyes.

"Please join me in the next room," Doris continued as she led the way.

Ethel ushered us into the kitchen where we had to crowd around the edges. This was because Doris had pulled four tables into the center and placed upon them dozens and dozens of cakes, all different shapes and sizes and with colorful icing. Doris put on a cake-spattered apron, as did Gracie. The aprons appeared to have been in some sort of icing explosion.

"We've had so much fun!" Gracie said. "I'm still on a sugar high." She peered at us, faking a wild stare.

"What is all this?" I asked.

"All this," said Doris, "is the taste-off."

"What exactly is a taste-off?" asked Lottie.

"Here are all the ideas I've had for Flora's wedding cake. Twenty-three, to be exact. We are going to spend the next hour trying each one to narrow down which cake Flora wants for her wedding."

"Now we're talking," said Ernie, picking up a fork.

Flora appeared bewildered. "I'm actually quite a plain person, Doris. I'd be happy with just a simple sponge cake and white icing."

Doris soured as she pointed her spatula at Flora. "Not on my watch, young lady," she said, wagging it up and down. "We can't have the people coming to your wedding think there might be something wrong with me. A simple sponge cake with white icing? They would think I was ill or dead. No, this is going to be the best cake that Southlea Bay has ever seen."

Flora's eyes widened with concern. "Please, I really don't want a lot of fuss." I watched her carefully. Her mood seemed to plummet as each day unfolded. It was as if she wanted to appear grateful but was really starting to feel suffocated by yet another way that Doris tried to "coordinate" her out of what she wanted.

Doris continued, undeterred. "OK, each of you take a plate and work your way around the cakes."

Lavinia stopped her incredulously. "You're telling us we're going to eat all these cakes?"

Annie shook her head, bemused. "I think I would end up in a diabetic coma."

"I'm not asking you to eat a slab," said Doris, annoyed. "Just a little bit here and a little bit there, and it's imperative that you take notes. I have a score sheet that I'll give to each of you, and you can give me marks out of ten on all the different areas—from taste, to texture, to how it looks."

Ernie beamed, flashing his gold teeth, his eyes agog as he took in the sights before him: a spread that would've put the Queen of England to shame. "Tell me where to start!" He lifted his fork in the air.

Doris placed a hand on his chest. "Start with your form," she said, giving him one to fill in.

"I can't eat a form," he retorted.

"No, but you need to make sure that you tell me which cakes you prefer."

"I prefer all of them," he added with a twinkle in his eye. "I just need to get going."

Ethel clicked her tongue with visible irritation.

Doris was having none of it. "Ernie, I will not let you lay one fork on any of these cakes until you agree to fill out this form."

"Well, when you put it like that," he said. "Yes, ma'am." He saluted her and took the form and a pen.

"OK," I said, grabbing myself a fork "Might as well get on with piling on the calories now. Glad I wore my stretch pants."

We all surrendered to Doris's leadership and moved around the table, taking heaping forkfuls of different cakes and marking down on our score sheets what we liked the best. Doris hovered over each of our shoulders as she made noises of encouragement and sometimes disapproval when people weren't filling their sheets in correctly.

As we continued to move around the kitchen, I noticed that Ernie wasn't really taking it very seriously; he was just ticking off boxes willy-nilly and pretending to give her his attention What he really seemed to be doing was enjoying cake.

"I made the fairy one," Gracie piped up, pointing to a tiered pink cake in the corner that was decorated with rainbow sparkles. On the top, she'd placed one of her crowns. "It's plain sponge and icing—like you want, Flora."

Flora smiled. "It looks lovely, Gracie."

"What is this?" Lavinia spit her cake back onto the plate.

Lottie admonished her sister, "Lavinia, that's not ladylike."

"Have you tried this one?" Lavinia pointed her spoon at a rather unassuming cake in the corner.

"That was an experiment," huffed Doris. "I take it you don't like it."

"Experiment with what?" asked Lavinia. "What you could use out of the garbage?"

"Just a few bits and pieces, you know, almond flour and prunes, and the likes of that," said Doris defensively. "I was getting bored by about three o'clock this morning. I'd already gone through pounds of flour when I decided to try this."

"I'm not sure what that was, but that is definitely not for me," said Lavinia, putting a big red X on her chart as she wiped her mouth. "It tastes like Chinese food."

"So that's where my sesame oil went," responded Doris thoughtfully. "I must have grabbed that instead of the canola oil by mistake."

We continued to make our rounds of the whole table. By the end of it, I was starting to feel quite sick.

"Well," said Doris, "do we have a winner?"

We all tallied up the marks, and Gracie's simple fairy cake with the pink icing won.

"I'm the winner," said Gracie, clapping her hands together.

"I don't believe it," said Doris. "After all this work I went to, you're going to go with something boring."

We all smiled. "Sorry, Doris," I said, "this is the one that tastes the best."

She huffed and collected the result sheets. "We'd better go and finish our book club meeting. Now, we know we've got plenty of cake. Which one would you like with your next cup of tea?"

"None!" We all shouted in unison.

CHAPTER NINE

JOHN WAYNE & THE WELSH SHEEPDOG TRIALS

I arrived at the wedding rehearsal early. I had more than one concern about Doris's wedding service ideas, and I wanted to be there to support Flora. As I walked into the Labettes' chapel, Ethel greeted me at the entrance She was set up at the door with a box of labels in her hand. Handing me one, she told me to write my name down.

Write my name down? I knew everybody and everybody knew me, but I did as I was told; I'd learned to do that the hard way.

I made my way into the room, which was stunning. What had looked like a sad, tired storage space just a short time before had been turned into a tiny chapel, especially with its vaulted ceilings, which were now repainted white It had lovely wood-paneled walls, and the huge picture window at the front gave me a stunning view of the water. The old exercise and gaming equipment was gone, and now the room was filled with lines of little wooden folding chairs, each one with a tapestry pillow made by the twins' mama warming its seats.

Down the center aisle, the twins had lit tall white candles, and the room smelled of fresh cedar and jasmine. As I made my way down the aisle, my feet creaking on the floorboards, I felt a sudden sense of excitement for Flora and her wedding. At the front of the aisle, the twins had placed a large vase of Christmas flowers and, dotted around the stage area, tiny poinsettias of white and pink.

I noticed that most members of the Rejected Writers' Book Club were already seated in the first few pews, awaiting our fearless leader. Everybody looked bemused and confused, each of them also wearing their labels. Lavinia's badge said "the Twin" and Lottie's said "the Other Twin." Ruby's read "Radical Nonconformist." Annie's read "the Dog Wrangler," and in Gracie's spidery hand, "Fairy."

Doris arrived in her full robes, wearing her label, which said "Wedding Coordinator and Reverend Doris Newberry."

When the door opened, Flora and Dan walked down the aisle together, hand in hand. Ethel followed after them, like a disenchanted bridesmaid, carrying her box of labels.

"They're not wearing their badges," she said with a sniff to Doris, who looked cross. Taking the badges from Ethel, she scribbled something on both of them and slapped a sticker onto Dan's chest that said "the Bridegroom" and then one onto Flora's that said "the Bride."

"Thank goodness," Dan joked. "I wouldn't have known who you were without your badge."

I shook my head as Flora smiled. She looked tired.

"It's better if everybody knows who they are," said Doris hotly as she encouraged everybody to move to the front of the aisle, where she had set up a large whiteboard with stick figures in different positions. She picked up a pointer, which she used to point to the stick figures on the board. Following a marked-out plan on the whiteboard, Doris said, "Right, let's take it from the top," as if we were all going to start high kicking in a line. Suddenly, she stopped. "Where's Martin?"

"He will be here any minute."

Doris's face displayed her annoyance. "The rehearsal was meant to be at five o'clock sharp. Did he not get the message?"

"Yeah, he did," I said, nodding, but he was not good at being told what to do.

Suddenly, he appeared at the door and waved to us all. Ethel ran up the aisle with the label box she'd snatched back from Doris.

When he joined the group, he was indeed wearing his name badge, which read "John Wayne." I shook my head. Doris complained, so he scribbled it out and wrote "Steve Martin" as a nod to the movie *Father of the Bride*. Doris was not amused.

"We have to get started now," she said. "Martin, you grab the bride. That's Flora." She pointed her stick at Flora's name tag.

I could see Martin's mouth already starting to twitch.

Doris started ordering everybody around. She was like an angry collie herding a flock at the Welsh sheepdog trials. She pointed her stick at Martin. "You take Flora"—she pointed back to Flora, who was standing next to Martin, then pointed to the chart—"up the aisle. Who's standing in for the best man?"

"That would be me," said Ruby, jumping up.

Suddenly, the doors opened again, and in walked a figure we all knew. "Olivia!" we shouted at once as she came down the aisle, her tiny birdlike figure draped in layers of black lace, her long dark hair rolling in coils down her back, and her usual bulky jewelry sparkling elegantly from her fingers. Olivia, my granddaughter's namesake, had been our music director for the musical we'd produced to try to save Annie's farm.

"I heard you'd be needing a pianist," she said and lifted her hands.

Reverend Doris huffed. "Olivia's agreed to help us out, and if she'd been on time, she'd have known."

Olivia raised her eyebrows and let them drop. She was not easily ruffled.

"For the wedding, I have Mrs. Hemlock, the local church

organist," Doris continued. "She will be playing the Wedding March." Flora nodded. "But for the rehearsal, she couldn't make it. They've got choir practice today. So I've asked Olivia to stand in. She will play the music for us."

Olivia slid past us all, making her way to the piano. I noticed she'd already been accosted by Ethel and was wearing her name tag, which said, "the One and Only Olivia."

That was true, all right.

"OK," said Doris, "hopefully, if we don't have any more interruptions, we can get this going." She pointed at her whiteboard again. "So, Martin"—she banged on it—"you take the bride"—she pointed at Flora—"to the top of the aisle." She pointed to the top of the aisle on her whiteboard.

"Think I've got it," said Martin, trying not to laugh.

"When the music starts, you, Ruby"—she pointed to the best man on the chart—"and you, Dan"—she caught him his her sights with her stick—"you will rise and wait for your bride. Annie and Ethel, you can stand in as the flower girl and ring bearer."

They both nodded as Annie put down her latest knitting project and Ethel grabbed her box of badges.

"You two will come down first, once the groom"—she swiveled her stick toward Dan— "and the best man"—she pointed to Ruby—"are standing. Got it?"

"I think so." Annie giggled. "I've been to a couple of weddings." She and Ethel moved to the back of the chapel.

"Then the bridesmaids will come down," Doris said and flicked her stick at Lavinia and Lottie.

"Maybe old maids would be more appropriate," Lottie said and sighed wistfully.

"You speak for yourself, sister dear," said Lavinia ruefully. "I'm considering picking up husband number four at this shindig."

"Do you know how to walk to the Wedding March?" inquired Doris, looking over her glasses.

"I might have done it a couple of times before," said Lavinia in her sassy fashion.

"And I've wore more than my fair share of bridesmaids dresses," added her sister in a weary tone.

"Go then," said Doris, banging her stick on the board.

And the sisters quickly scooted up the aisle to take their places.

"OK," said Doris. "Let's do it. Places, everybody. Hit it, Olivia." She pointed her stick at Olivia.

Olivia started to play "Ragtime," and Doris gave her a cold, hard stare. "Just making sure you're all awake," Olivia said and then slid gracefully into "Wedding March."

Doris pointed at Dan, who, trying not to smirk, stood up next to Ruby. Then she motioned to Annie. Annie decided to play her part to the full. She danced down the aisle, scattering fake petals and humming as she went. Doris looked stolidly at Annie as she watched her giggle and twirl into one of the pews. Ethel, on the other hand, was very reverent. She used her name tag badge box, pretending it was the ring cushion, and she walked somberly down the aisle. Doris nodded her approval, and she, too, slid into one of the rows.

Lavinia started making her way down the aisle, batting her eyelashes and waving at imaginary people.

"What in heck's name are you doing?" hissed her sister, walking a couple of paces behind her. "This is not some ticker-tape parade."

"Practicing," responded her sister through a beaming smile. "He's out there somewhere."

Doris shook her head sternly as the sisters reached the front. She pointed her pointer at Martin. "Go, bride," she said.

Flora and Martin started to walk down the aisle.

"Stop," Doris shouted.

Both of them stopped, shocked.

"You're walking too fast, Flora. You need to step together.

Step together. It needs to be slow and graceful. Remember, you're a bride."

Flora shook her head, and I saw Martin tap her on the arm reassuringly.

"Go again," said Doris.

Olivia's hands came down on the keys once more. Flora started to move forward again.

"Stop," shouted Doris. "What are you doing, Flora?"

"Trying to walk down the aisle," she responded, obviously frustrated.

"Well, you're not walking on the beat, are you?"

"I'm trying," she said, getting irritated.

Doris huffed, put down her pointer, and marched up the aisle. Pushing Martin aside, she took hold of Flora's arm and showed her how to walk on the beat. When Doris left and went back to the front, Flora seemed perturbed.

"Go," she shouted.

I could see that Flora was really struggling. She tried it two more times before she eventually got it the way that Doris liked it. By the time she got to the front of the aisle, she looked totally rattled.

Doris looked out at the invisible crowd and started the service:

"Ladies and gentlemen, a wise old cook once said there's more to a good ham-hock stew than the trotters you put in it."

Flora stopped her. "What are you doing?"

"The service," said Doris abruptly.

"That's not our service," Flora responded, blinking behind her glasses.

"Yes, well, I've changed the one that you did," Doris said defensively. "It wasn't very good the way it was written. Lots of flowery words and sad dead poet references. You surely don't want to talk about dead people at your wedding. I think something more down-to-earth is better. So I'm comparing getting married to preparing my favorite pig trotter stew recipe. This will be better."

I bit my lip, trying to decide if I should jump in and rescue her, as Flora appeared taken aback. Before I could respond, Flora spoke again, her voice raised.

"B-but those were the words of some of the most romantic poets—Keats, Lord Byron, and William Wordsworth," she stammered on.

"All dead," said the Reverend sharply, straightening her dog collar and adding, "I looked them up on the World Wide Web. I've also changed your vows," she added. "Here's your copy of each of them. I think we should be consistent, don't you?"

Flora read the words in front of her. "What is all this about baking and marriage? I was using passages from *Shakespeare's Sonnets.*"

"He's dead, too!" retorted Doris.

Flora looked devastated, and she glanced at Dan, who lowered his tone. "I will fight for this if you don't want it, but just so you know, whatever you say to me, I don't care," he said. "As long as you say 'I do' at the end."

But Flora was having none of it.

"I want my Shakespeare," she said through her gritted teeth.

Doris huffed. "OK, if you insist, you can do a little bit of that Shakespeare stuff but then do some of this as well," she said as she slapped her stick on the page that she'd written.

We carried on through the rest of the rehearsal—with Doris pushing us around—until, eventually, it was over. I noted Flora appeared frustrated and tired. I took her aside.

"You can do your own vows, Flora. Don't let Doris boss you around. Just say whatever you want on the day. She can't stop you."

Flora nodded, but I could see that she had had different expectations of the rehearsal, and she left looking frustrated.

"I think that went well," said Doris, straightening her robes. "I think it will go great next week."

We left the church. I caught Martin's eye. He whistled. "I'm glad she wasn't around when we got married," he said. "I may never have waited at the end of that aisle."

"I may never have come down it," I added, smiling as he gave me a hug.

"Yes, she missed her career opportunity all right," Martin continued. "As a divorce mediator, she could have halved the divorce rate by now."

"How come?" I asked.

"No one would have ever gotten married."

~

JOHN SAT in his car outside the gates at the Labettes' house, hoping Flora would be walking home this evening. He was getting antsy. For the last two weeks, he had tried to talk to Flora alone, but she was always with Dan or one of these ladies. As he saw Dan drive her away in his car, he made a decision. He was going to make one last-ditch attempt to confront her. He had heard from Lavinia that there was going to be a bachelorette party at Doris's. He was going to talk to her then and tell her what he knew about her. He checked the letter he had written the night before; it was still in his pocket. When he got a chance, he would go down to the post office and get the stamps he needed. If for some reason he didn't get to talk to her this time, he was going to post this to her, and she could send the money he wanted on to him.

CHAPTER TEN

CLUCKING HENS & A DRESS UNFIT FOR
A BRIDE

Not to be outdone again by the Labette sisters, Doris insisted on throwing Flora's bachelorette party at her house. When I arrived, I was amazed to see everybody sitting in the front room, wearing a crazy hat. What was it with Doris and hats? Only the year before, she had made us all wear odd hats to help inspire us for our show. Here we were again, everyone sitting in their usual array of odd chairs, looking very strange.

"Did I miss the memo?" I asked.

"Come in quickly," said Doris, hustling me into a chair and shoving a hat on my head. As she raced off to a different room, I looked at the group. They were wearing hats with bird pictures decorating the sides.

"There's one thing you can say for small towns," said Lavinia. "You never get bored."

"Amen," said Lottie.

"I feel sorry for those poor schmucks who live in a city where they have real issues to deal with on a daily basis," added Ruby, shaking her head.

Gracie clapped her hands. "I love my hat! A tinsel crown is my favorite, but I do like being a bird."

I took off my hat to get a closer look at it. I thought it was some sort of fowl—a duck or a goose. It looked as if Doris had drawn them herself.

"I helped color them in," added Gracie. "And I added the sparkles."

I looked again at my hat. There were definitely plenty of sparkles.

Doris arrived back in the room. "She's here, she's here. Get ready."

"Get ready for what?" I asked.

"We're going to all surprise her. I've got many surprises planned tonight. It's going to be fun," she added sternly, without making it sound fun at all.

Doris raced off into the hallway.

"I always get nervous when she talks about fun," said Lavinia. "I remember all the other days when we've had Doris's 'fun.' 'Fun' going to see a publisher all the way in San Francisco. 'Fun' putting on a show when none of us could actually dance or sing. Doris's idea of fun is very different than mine."

Suddenly, the living-room door opened and we all stood there, not quite sure what to do. But instead of Flora, it was John. Doris looked really disappointed.

"It was only him," she said, pushing him into the front room. "He was lurking around outside."

"I just wanted a quick word with Flora—" he said . . . then stopped. He surveyed the room, taking in the group of middle-aged women sitting in duck hats with sparkles.

"Don't ask," I said, reading his expression. I could only imagine what he was thinking. "Just roll with it. I've realized that with Doris, that's the best way to go."

John's face was a cross between *you all look crazy* and *what did I get myself into now?*

Doris sat John down in an empty chair before he had time to protest. "You have to stay here before we start the party. I can't risk you leaving while we're waiting for Flora to arrive. It might spoil the surprise." She handed him a hat.

He looked at her as though she'd asked him to eat dirt.

"Well, put it on, put it on," said Doris, hustling him along. There was something about Doris when she was in her organizational mode that could rival any dictator. You just felt forced to do whatever she said. I noted this as John shoved his hat on his head and sat there, looking confused. He would certainly have some stories to take back to the city when he finally disentwined himself from small-town madness.

As Doris disappeared to continue her watch at the kitchen window, Ethel rolled a tray of tea and one of Doris's cakes in. She was the most depressing bird I'd ever seen.

Suddenly, there was a yell from the kitchen.

"She's here, it's definitely her," said Doris. She stomped back into the room and signaled to Ethel to answer the door. As Ethel plodded off to follow her orders, Doris informed us of the plan. "As soon as she comes in, we all need to jump up and start clucking."

"Start what?" said Lottie.

"Clucking," reiterated Doris.

"Ah, they're hens," I said, realizing what the picture on the hat was.

"Yes, cluck—like a hen," she added, as if explaining it to a group of kindergartners.

I smiled at John, who looked bewildered.

"Welcome to Small Town," I said. "I expect a month ago, you couldn't imagine jumping up and clucking like a hen."

Flora appeared in the front room, and we all jumped up and started clucking, even John, though I must say, his attempt was rather half-hearted.

Flora looked as though she couldn't connect the dots.

"Surprise!" shouted Doris over the barnyard din.

"Surprise?" inquired Flora. "You're right, I'm surprised. I didn't expect to find a brood of hens in here."

"I gave it so much gusto," said Annie. "I almost laid an egg." She giggled.

"We have one for you," said Gracie, picking up a large hen hat and placing it on Flora's head. "You can be the queen hen."

"Is there a reason I'm a barnyard animal?" asked Flora. She looked drained and tired. The wedding preparations were obviously having an effect on her. That, and having to battle Doris on a daily basis couldn't be a happy prospect, I thought to myself.

"Isn't it obvious?" snapped Doris.

We all stared back blankly.

"It's a hen night," shouted Gracie.

"A hen night?" we asked in unity, even John.

"Oh yes," said Gracie. "We had them in England all the time."

"Is that like a bachelorette party?" I asked.

"Yes, it's the British version. We call it a *hen night*. It's a night where we all celebrate the bride-to-be."

"Ah!" I said. The dots were finally joining up together. "This is some sort of British tradition. I guess they have Small Town over there as well?"

"Yes," said Gracie. "I'm from one."

"That makes sense," I responded.

"This is just the start of the adventure," added Doris, jumping to her feet. "We are all going to celebrate Flora's wedding, and we're all going to be hens, except John. He'll have to go, as this is for female hens only—no roosters."

John did not look unhappy about that prospect. "No problem," he said, whipping the hat off his head and leaving. *One escaped*, I thought. Shame Martin wasn't here; he'd quite have enjoyed something like this.

"OK, Doris," I said, "lay it on us. What's the plan?"

"I've put together a very special event," said Doris. "I have managed to talk people all over town into helping me with this plot. "There are surprises hidden everywhere. We are going to cluck our way around town, collecting each one and celebrating Flora along the way."

"Cluck around, collecting surprises?" I cringed. "Sounds like a blast."

"Good," said Doris. "I thought you'd enjoy it."

"Lead on, Macduff," said Lavinia, leaping to her feet, readjusting her hen hat, and putting on her jacket.

"First stop," said Doris, "is Ruby-Skye's shop. Now, everyone has to keep wearing their hats. Let's all stay in the party mood."

"I wouldn't dream of getting out of the party mood," I said sarcastically.

"We'll buddy up in cars, and we'll meet you there," she continued. "I have an exceptional surprise waiting for you, Flora. I know you're going to love it."

Flora, I noticed, hadn't said much since she'd arrived. Now she stared blankly back at Doris with not even a hint of enthusiasm on her face.

"I can't be out long tonight," she said wearily. "I've got a lot going on, you know. Lots still to organize."

"Absolutely," said Doris. "This shouldn't take us longer than about four hours."

Four hours! I thought. Four hours dressed as a hen, clucking around town. All my days in California and cocktail parties loomed large in my memory. What was I thinking, moving to the Northwest? What was I thinking, moving to a small town?

"Off we go," said Doris. "Go get in your cars, and we'll meet at Ruby's in twenty minutes." As we started to move out of the room, Doris stopped us. "We have to cluck."

What came next was a cacophony of pathetic clucking noises from us all—except for Annie and Gracie, who seemed to really be into the spirit of the thing. Ruby-Skye had managed to balance her hen hat on top of the turban she was wearing. It looked quite regal there.

"I can take a couple in my car," I said.

"I'm with you," said Ruby.

"Me, too," said Annie.

And we got into our cars, clucking as we went, and drove into town.

Doris's first stop with her brood was, indeed, at Ruby-Skye's Wool Emporium.

"I'm not sure she's gonna like this," Ruby murmured.

She opened up the store, and Ruby turned on the lights. In the center of the shop was a mannequin wearing a dated white satin wedding dress. It looked vintage, from the '50s or the '60s. It was a large, bulky size to make room for large breasts and thick hips. We all stood there, rooted to the spot.

"Here we go," said Doris, as she and Ethel stood on either side of the mannequin and stretched out their hands like a pair of misfit Vanna Whites. "Just what you always wanted." Doris swept her hand down the dress, as if that would add some chic to it.

Lavinia put a pink-nailed finger to her lips. "Oh, my," she said. "You could get three Floras in that. Or two twins. Or just one Doris."

Horrified, Flora stuttered, "Wha-what exactly is this?"

"I saw how much you didn't like the dirty white dress that posh shop put together for you, so I thought I would do you a great service and let you use the wedding dress that I got married to my husband in, God rest his soul. It's very classy. It came out of the Sears catalog."

"I already have a wedding dress," said Flora, mortified.

"But it's the wrong color," answered Doris, annoyed. "I think you should at least try this on. We've gone to a lot of trouble to get this ready. Ruby has said that she will alter it for you. I know you don't have a mother to pass a dress down to you, so I thought this was the next best thing."

Flora's features softened for a moment as she appeared to contemplate Doris's words. Her expression mixed: there was sudden sadness at the mention of her mom but also some realization that Doris, as bombastic as she was, often had a heart-centered motivation for her actions. We had seen evidence of it when she led us all to California to save Gracie's reputation and when she had worked flat out to save Annie's farm.

Before Flora could respond, Doris bustled over to her side and started ushering her toward a makeshift changing room.

Lavinia's eyes went skyward. "Maybe we should have hit the bar first," she whispered to me. "This would have been a lot more entertaining if we were all drunk."

Flora did not look impressed as Ethel managed to pull the dress off the mannequin, drape it carefully over her arms, and walk to the fitting room. I shook my head. This wasn't going to be good. Two minutes later, Flora waded out in the huge dress.

I couldn't help myself. I needed to say something. "Doris," I said, "that dress is—"

She cut me off.

"Stunning," said Doris, finishing my sentence with her own delusion.

"I need to get a pair of her glasses," said Lavinia.

Red faced and frustrated, Flora moved into the middle of the shop, where Doris and Ethel started grabbing at bits of fabric and pulling them in.

"What if we were to add some tucks in here?" Doris asked Ruby-Skye.

"Mm-hmm," said Ruby-Skye. "Yep, that would do it. Tucks—that's all it would need." Her tone was sarcastic.

"I really don't think this is me," said Flora as bits of her fell out of different corners of the dress. She tried to pull it up onto her shoulders but it wouldn't stay.

"I think it could be great," said Doris, screwing up her eyes. "What do you think, Ruby?"

I looked at Ruby, who pushed her chicken hat to the side.

"I think it's up to Flora," she said.

"Let's just pin her in it and we'll see," added Doris.

Ruby looked uncomfortably at Flora but finally did Doris's bidding and pinned in the sides. By the time she finished, the dress was completely misshapen the enormous bosoms folding in a *V* at the front like a flap and the waist now dropped to her knees, like something out of the 1920s.

"Maybe we could pull it up by the shoulders," said Doris, grabbing hold of the top of the dress and lifting it up, making Flora look like some sort of crazy wedding puppet.

Somebody could do with being pulled up by the shoulders, I thought and then said aloud, "Why don't we let Flora think about it? We'll take it off her for now. At least it's given her another choice. Right, Flora?"

Flora looked fit to burst. "I don't need another choice," she growled.

"I know," I whispered.

Flora took off the dress—or, more realistically, she breathed in and it fell to her ankles.

"Well," said Doris, "we need to cluck our way over to the florist. I have big surprises over there."

Flora reddened.

"Oh, it's a Doris-style fun night for sure," said Lottie quietly to the rest of us. "I'm already praying that nobody dies."

Leaving the Wool Emporium, we clucked reluctantly over to the florist, where Mrs. Bickerstaff was having a late Thursday night. She looked exasperated when she saw everybody come in.

"Doris Newberry," she said. "I've got a note in here slipped under my door that Flora might be considering changing her flowers and that you would like to put an order in for her."

Flora stared at Doris, mortified.

"Did you put the bouquet together I requested on my note?" said Doris grumpily.

Mrs. Bickerstaff pulled out the bouquet of bright yellow and orange flowers.

"Yellow and orange?" said Annie. "I thought you were going with pink and mauve?"

"I am," said Flora through gritted teeth.

"Look how bright these are," said Doris as she held them up to Flora's face. "They bring out your complexion."

Sure do, I thought as I looked at the fuming bride-to-be. *If red is the color Doris is trying to match.*

"Are you sure you don't want to go with these colors instead?" Doris continued airily.

Once again, Ethel put her hand up, Vanna White style, as if to help present them.

Flora slammed down the flowers.

"No, I think I'll stick with my original colors because I've already bought all the reels of ribbon to go with it," she said smartly.

Tensions were starting to build, so I decided to defuse the situation.

"Listen, this is a lovely idea for you to put this bird party on for Flora," I said. "But you know what? I think we probably should go over to the Crab and have a drink and something to eat? Have a little break in between some of these great ideas you have, Doris."

Everyone nodded their agreement, even Doris.

The whole barnyard clucked across the street to the Crab Apple Diner. Gladys came around the corner just as we arrived, clucking our way through the door. She took one look at the lot of us, turned on her heels, and disappeared back into the restaurant.

Impatient, Doris rang a little bell that was on the welcome desk.

Two minutes later, Gladys was back. "I thought for a moment I'd had a hallucination. The chef has been cooking all these new mushrooms and I thought maybe there was something funny about them, but then I realized it was you people," she said shaking her head. "Why should I be surprised if you're all standing here looking like a bunch of chickens? Where would you like to roost today?"

"Usual booth," said Doris in a high, henlike voice.

Gladys blinked at her twice and shook her head. "Waddle this way." She grabbed a handful of menus.

We made our way to the booth, some of us clucking a lot less quietly than the others.

"Will you be eating?" asked Gladys. "Or just pecking on some corn?"

"We'll be eating," said Doris, nodding. "I have made special arrangements with that new chef. You can bring out the party fare she has been working on for me."

I smiled to myself. The chef had actually been working at the Crab for nearly two years, but since the last chef had been here for twenty-five years, she was still known as "the new chef." *This small town,* I thought.

"Interesting," said Gladys. "Eating and the new chef don't always go together. Most of what she creates is like art. Nobody actually wants to eat it. It just needs to be stared at. In the meantime, I'll get you some drinks. What would you like?"

We all put in our drinks order, and Doris started an obviously rehearsed monologue. Taking hold of Flora's hand, she gripped it tightly, saying, "Flora, this is where it all started. This is where we decided to go on the road trip. That day back on our road trip, none of us had any idea that in a few days you'd meet your husband."

Flora actually started to tear up.

"Now that your flowers are sorted out," said Doris, making a check on the clipboard, "and your dress is decided, all we need to do now is figure out the food."

"The food," said Flora.

"Oh, and the band," said Doris, looking at her board.

"I'm already having Happy Weddings Catering Service take care of my food," said Flora.

"I know," said Doris. "I saw that you'd written that down, but I know you wanted help. And when I talked to them, they were very awkward, not very pleasant to deal with at all. So I've decided to take care of the catering for you. There are plenty of little recipes for snips and snaps that will work."

"Snips and snaps," echoed Lavinia. "Doesn't sound very wedding-ish."

"Well, you know, just little bits and pieces that I'll throw together—sausage and cheese and eggs in little puff-pastry bases."

"But I was doing an organic buffet," said Flora. "I have it all color coordinated."

"I can make it colorful," said Doris defensively. "I'll throw in some tomatoes here and there, maybe some beets."

"Beets, tomato and sausage," said Ruby, screwing up her eyes.

"Can we have ice cream, too?" said Gracie, clapping her hands together.

"Yes, Mama, we can have ice cream just for you. We could have 'confetti' flavor, that's very wedding-ish." Doris, getting excited, wrote it down on her clipboard. "I'll create all this for half the price. Don't you worry. No one's going to go hungry at one of my affairs. And I talked to the band for you." Doris added, looking up from her list.

"They took six months to book," said Flora frantically. She was starting to lose her temper. "What did you do to my band?"

"I didn't do anything to them," said Doris defensively. "I just realized that they're not quite what you're going for."

"They're the best we have on the Island," said Flora, her volume escalating. Around the restaurant, people stopped eating and looked toward our table.

"I have that group of bongo players. I've come up with some lively, upbeat wedding tempos for them. You know, Calypso wedding tunes and such. I told them to bring their drums. Flora, this is going to be a lot cheaper for you and so much classier. Don't you worry, I've got it all in hand."

Flora suddenly jumped up from the table, slammed down her hand, and shouted, "That's it! Doris Newberry, stop interfering with my wedding!"

We all stared at her, mute. I don't think I'd ever heard Flora raise her voice. "This is my wedding—*my* wedding—and I'm going to do it my way."

To emphasize her point, she pulled off her hen hat and threw it down on the table.

Every eye was drawn down to the abandoned paper chicken lying deflated in front of us. Flora apparently meant business.

It was just then that Dan arrived, breathless. I thought Flora was going to burst into tears.

"Dan," she said, throwing herself into his arms.

"Uh, hello there. What a bunch of cute chicks." He smiled at the group over her shoulder.

Flora seemed embarrassed. "It's some sort of British tradition," she said dismissively.

"I'm so glad you're here," he said and seemed like he was excited about something. "Look who's just arrived."

From behind him came two people we remembered from the road trip: Dan's parents. We all got up to give them a hug.

"Hello to you all," said his mom. "So glad to see you all again. Can't wait for the wedding. We've brought a childhood friend of Dan's. She said she knew you all and was very enthusiastic about coming along to share the experience."

Someone else sauntered in.

It was Marcy.

She had not been back to town since trying to break up Flora and Dan's relationship the year before. And I realized all at once that Dan's parents probably didn't have a clue of all the trouble she'd caused for Dan and Flora before they had invited her along.

Flora's face turned from red to purple. This, I was guessing, was the last straw.

"Hello, everyone," said Marcy airily with a sweep of her hand. "So glad I could make it out for this little affair. I wouldn't miss Danny's wedding for anything," she said, stroking Dan's hands seductively. He looked dumbstruck. "I have some news to share."

Pulling off one of her cashmere gloves, she flashed her hand in front of us, and there was the largest diamond I had ever seen. We all stared, our mouths agape.

Gladys shuffled back to the table with two trays of very odd-looking food.

"Apparently, this is what you ladies are eating tonight, something that the new chef calls 'snips and snaps.' Looks more like snips and snails to me. I've been looking for the puppy dog tails on the way over here." Gladys caught a glimpse of what Marcy was flashing. She whistled. "Wow, that's some rock you got yourself, there. Whose arm did you twist into buying you that?"

Ignoring her, Marcy ran her hand through her silky blonde hair. "I'm getting married to an old childhood friend, Jason. Do you remember him, Danny? Jason Hamilton. He's now a merchant banker."

There was silence from the table.

Dan looked taken aback. "Jason? Wow. Yes, of course, I remember him. You and Jason? I'm so pleased for you. Isn't that great everyone?" he said, encouraging us all as he tried to thaw the hens on ice.

We all absently nodded our chicken heads in response.

"We're going to have a spectacular wedding," Marcy continued. "On his yacht. I'm in the planning stages right now. I have twenty bridesmaids, and I'll arrive at the beach in a horse-drawn carriage, and he'll arrive in his brand-new white Lamborghini. Then he'll travel to his yacht on his speedboat, and my bridesmaids and I will be rowed out by Hawaiian groomsmen. We're going to have native flower girls, who will sail ahead of us, dancing and sprinkling exotic petals for us to sail through. We will hold the ceremony on the yacht under a canopy woven with a thousand more exotic flowers and indigenous fruit then afterward, in a grand marquee on the beach, we'll eat lobster and drink from champagne fountains."

We all blinked. Flora sat down hard, her gaze fixed on her bird hat. I could see the disappointment in her face. Marcy was on some sort of Princess Diana–style wedding kick when Flora, just ten minutes before, had been wearing Doris's old wedding dress and then fighting off a bouquet of ugly orange and yellow flowers. I knew she was probably thinking this wasn't what she'd planned for the night.

"Would you like to join us?" Annie asked, in a tone that suggested she hoped Marcy would decline.

"Oh, no," said Marcy. "I have to get back to my hotel. There are so many arrangements I'm still making online. Just wanted to make sure you all knew you had an invitation to the wedding in Maui."

"Maui?" Annie whistled. "Isn't that off the island?" she asked sarcastically.

"Great to see you all," Marcy said unconvincingly and then kissed Dan seductively on the cheek as she headed out with his parents in tow.

Dan squeezed Flora's arm.

"I should get Mom and Dad settled into their hotel." And he, too, was gone.

We all looked down at the tray of Play-Doh that was disguised as food. Nobody seemed to be feeling very hungry.

Flora stood up. "I have to go," she said in a very calm manner that surprised us all. "I'm exhausted."

"I can come with you, Flora," I offered, wondering if she needed some support.

"No," she said sharply. "I would like to be alone."

With that, she left the restaurant, the brood, and her chicken hat on the table behind her.

~

ARRIVING HOME LATE THAT NIGHT, Flora was drained and close to tears. She closed the door and leaned against it. In front of her, on the mat, was a wedding card addressed to her. Sighing deeply, she crouched down and picked it up.

CHAPTER ELEVEN

DISAPPEARING BRIDES & BAILEYS FOR BREAKFAST

John had a terrible night's sleep. He had a nightmare about seeing Flora coming down the aisle, and when she lifted her veil, Dan was shocked and stopped the wedding to ask her what was going on. She turned to the church congregation and pointed to John, saying, "It was his fault."

John tried to shout back in his sleep, but he had lost his voice. Nothing came out. He finally woke up in a heavy sweat and sat up in the bed. That's when he realized it was just a nightmare, but he knew exactly what it meant. He wasn't going to do it. He couldn't. He didn't know what he'd been thinking. He wasn't malicious. He'd actually become quite fond of Flora. He just couldn't hurt her in this way. She was OK.

He got out of bed, went to the hall closet, and pulled out his jacket. He was going to burn it. He'd made up his mind. That was what he would do: burn the letter and give her the document right now so he couldn't go back on his word. So he could move forward with a new life.

He reached into his inside pocket to recover the letter. It was gone. He scoured through all of his pockets but, except for a pack of cigarettes and the candy cane he had been given the first day, they were empty.

He couldn't believe it.

It was gone.

≈

EVEN THOUGH IT was still a few days before the wedding, the Labette sisters couldn't wait any longer. They had to give Flora their gift, and they had to give it to her now. She'd mentioned she had a nine a.m. appointment at the Bob and Curl so Sadie could deep condition her hair.

Lavinia picked up an elegant box and placed it in the trunk. When they arrived at the Bob and Curl at exactly 9:15, Sadie was on the telephone, a concerned look on her face. Lavinia slipped in and smiled, waiting for Sadie to hang up before saying, "Sorry to bother you, honey. We just wanted a quick minute with the bride-to-be."

Sadie nodded as she hung up. "You and me both."

Lavinia knotted her brows. "I thought Flora had an appointment here this morning."

"She did, but she didn't turn up. In fact, that's who I was just calling."

"That doesn't sound like Flora," added Lottie by Lavinia's side, voicing everyone's concern.

"I know," said Sadie. "I would pop over and check on her, but I have a color coming in at nine thirty and I need to be here."

"Probably just a case of pre-wedding jitters," said Lottie, trying to stay optimistic. "Lavinia threw up all morning before she got married to her third husband, Hank. Didn't you, Lavinia?"

"Yes, I did, dear, but I think the name of that was *sheer terror.* My stomach had realized what it took my mind another six months to figure out: that I should never have married that blasted man."

"Lavinia!" screeched Lottie in her high-pitched altar tone. "There's no need for profanity."

Sadie smiled at the sisters, obviously charmed.

Lavinia continued, "Why don't we just pop across the road and see about Flora? If she's jittery, I have a fabulous family recipe that can cure all manner of ailments. It has a good amount of booze in it, which seems to calm the jitters right down."

Lottie tapped her sister's hand. "We'll have none of our old family concoctions here. The last thing Flora needs first thing in the morning is alcohol. We will pop over there, though, just to make sure she is OK."

Carrying their pretty package, the Labettes made their way up Main Street and onto the little side street where Flora's tiny cottage sat. After opening the wrought iron gate and moving to the doorstep, they knocked on the door.

~

JOHN DROVE into town like someone possessed by the devil. He had to find that letter before anyone picked it up and passed it on to Flora. He felt ashamed to think he'd even thought of doing such a thing. He would start where he had parked at the bank and retrace his steps.

He pulled into a parking space and jumped out of the car, forgetting to even lock it. Being in Southlea Bay had started to rub off on him. He walked up the road toward the post office, his eyes fixed only on the ground. He didn't want to miss it. It had to be here somewhere. But his heart continued to sink as he saw nothing.

He arrived at the red-brick building and rushed inside, glancing frantically around. Mrs. Barber had just opened the door and was humming as she readied herself for her day. John went straight to her.

"Did you find an envelope yesterday?"

Mrs. Barber didn't seem to notice his desperate face or the fact that he seemed in an awful rush. She just said, "Well, good morning. John, isn't it? What a lovely morning."

He tried again. "A letter, Mrs. Barber. Did you by any chance find a letter?"

She laughed and nodded. "I find lots of post, John. They're in my sacks in the back. I have a post office. This is my business."

"No," he said, "this is very important." He seized her wobbly round shoulders and pulled her toward him. She bristled a little, as if it wasn't post office procedure to be grabbed, in particular by a young man from out of town.

"It was addressed to Flora. Do you have a letter for Flora?"

She released herself from his grip and stepped behind the desk, as if she needed to remind him of her authority. "I have lots of letters and of course some for Flora."

"But did you find one on the floor? I might have dropped it."

She sniffed. "We have a box for that. I will go and look." She moved into the back office.

~

DORIS NEWBERRY WAS WOUND UP. She planned on going over to Flora's to discuss more wedding suggestions. She put on her shoes and started to make her way to the door when someone knocked. It was Ethel.

"Here is the book you lent me," she said in a tight voice. Wearing her usual dour expression, she continued, "It was very good. Very funny." She said the word *funny* as if she'd just sucked an extra-hot jalapeno right out of the jar. "I should let you know that I saw your momma wandering back toward town when I was on the bus. She has on her slippers and a chemise housecoat."

Doris puffed out her cheeks. This wasn't going to be a good day—she could feel it. "Come on, Ethel. We have a mission in town. We can pick up Mama on the way." Doris picked up her car keys, slipped on her town shoes, and closed the door.

Doris found her mama walking along the road, singing "Kumbaya." She pulled up next to her and rolled down the window. "Mama, what are you doing?"

"I'm just taking a stroll, Dotty dear," she said. "I thought I would drop off this little sign I'd made for Dan and Flora. 'Your happily ever after has just begun.'" She uncovered the sign that she'd made, draped in pink polka dot tissue paper.

Doris sighed. "Get in, Mama. I'm on my way to Flora's now. I'll give you a lift."

"Lovely!" Gracie jumped into the car.

~

LAVINIA LABETTE STOOD, peeking into Flora's window, reporting her findings to her sister below her. "There are open boxes laid on the table with lots of lovely blue-and-green tissue paper, as if she'd opened it and pulled something out to wear. Oh! Looks expensive. Like the box that comes from Macy's. You know, like the one I bought that lovely camel-colored suit for us in?"

"I don't care about a suit." Lottie rubbed her hands together, nervously. "Tell me if you see Flora."

"Well, no," she answered, "but it looks dark and disheveled in there. Actually, very un-Flora-like. She's usually quite a tidy Heidi."

"Lord," cried Lottie, throwing her hands up to heaven. "Please let her be OK. God, please send us a soldier of the Lord to help us."

"Stop your wailing," said Lavinia. "There's probably a perfectly good reason she's not here. A girl could be a thousand different places a few days before her wedding."

~

MRS. BARBER CAME BACK to the front desk and appeared to balk at the fact that John was still standing there. She took off her reading glasses and stuck them into her hair. They sat there, caught firmly in the mangled nest with a couple of other pairs. "Now," she said in her polite, but businesslike voice, "there is nothing in the box. When did you lose it?"

John shook his head in disbelief. "Yesterday. I told you, I dropped an envelope somewhere in town. It was addressed to Flora."

"Oh yes," said Mrs. Barber, distracted. "Sweet Flora is getting married. She's been getting all kinds of mail." Suddenly, the light bulb appeared to go off in her mind. She started to giggle. "Oh, that's what you're talking about." Then she added, reassuringly, "Don't worry, young man. I found your card on the floor, under the parcel table. It didn't have a stamp on it, but I was passing Flora's cottage on my way home and thought it was a wedding card for her. I just popped it through her door. I wanted to make sure she got it before the wedding—"

Before she could finish her sentence, he raced from the building.

~

I FOUGHT exhaustion after another restless morning with twin two-year-olds; I didn't know how Stacy did it. I actually left early for work at the library just to gather myself. As I made my way up the Main Street hill, an odd sight caught my eye: Lavinia Labette was standing up on one of Flora's garden benches, peeking into the window. I stopped the car and got out. As I reached Flora's gate, John ran up beside me, out of breath. The wrought iron gateway squealed, announcing our arrival.

"Ah, here are John and Janet," said Lottie. "Praise the Lord.

God has answered my prayer. Maybe John can climb into one of the windows or something."

Suddenly, Doris pulled up beside the house, and three more ladies got out and approached the door. "Why, here are Doris, Ethel, and Gracie," said Lottie.

Lavinia put her hand on her hip and looked at her sister. "Lottie, dear, you really need to be less fervent in your prayers for help. You ask God to send us a soldier and he sends us a whole platoon!"

Lottie's eyes twinkled. She was always excited when God answered her prayers. As we assembled on Flora's step, Lavinia brought us up to date on the hairdressing appointment and the disheveled front room.

"Stand aside," Doris said in her authoritarian tone. She reached below a plant pot, pulled out a single spare key, and put it into the lock.

Lottie rubbed her hands together. "Do you think it's a good idea to go in like this? She may have only gone for a walk or shopping. I hate to intrude."

I took her hand to calm her. "We're just checking. It's not like Flora to miss a hairdressing appointment, especially so close to her wedding. Maybe she's sick. We should at least go in and find out."

John's face paled.

We all walked into the darkened house. It was chilled, devoid of life or warmth. It had obviously been without heat all night. As I looked around the room, everything was disorganized, as if someone had left in a hurry: A tray of tea on the table with a used tea bag. Shoes were strewn on the floor and clothes thrown across the chairs.

Lottie called up the stairs toward Flora's room and slowly, tentatively, made her way up. Suddenly, the phone rang and everybody jumped.

Lavinia picked it up. "Hello?" she said reluctantly. then: "Oh, hello, Dan. How are you? Flora? You want to speak to Flora?" Lavinia faltered.

Everyone in the room stared at her, waiting.

"No, I'm afraid she's not available right now. I'll get her to call you when she is. Uh-huh. Good-bye."

We all stood there for a minute before Doris broke the silence. "Why didn't you ask him if he'd seen her?"

"I didn't want to worry the poor boy, for goodness sake," said Lavinia. "If he just called, it means he doesn't know she isn't here, which means we have to figure this out before we worry him half to death."

Lottie returned from the bedroom as pale as John. She reached out and took my hand to steady herself. She tried to sit down.

"What is it?" asked Doris, noticing her ashen expression. "What's wrong?"

She swallowed and then said, "Flora's gone. I checked her bedroom. There are clothes out on the bed, and her favorite travel bag is gone."

"That doesn't mean anything," said Lavinia. "She may just be half-packed for her honeymoon."

Before Lavinia could continue, I realized something. "Haven't you noticed something else? Mr. Darcy isn't here. He never leaves the house. I don't know where or why, but I think you're right. She's gone."

There was a long silence as everyone took in that information.

"I hope it wasn't anything we did," whispered Lottie, the worry obvious in her tone. "Maybe she really wanted to have her wedding in the community hall after all."

"That can't be it," her sister interjected. "It's more likely that god-awful dress or the terrible wedding service Doris was trying to inflict on her that sent her over the edge."

Doris stiffened and barked back, "What was wrong with my

dress? I thought Flora would want to be married in white. There was nothing wrong with that dress that a nip and tuck wouldn't have solved."

"Nip and tuck," Lavinia railed back. "It was huge. We could have added tent poles to the edges and hosted the wedding breakfast under it."

Annie shook her head. "It was probably more to do with the flowers." She then added pointedly, "Flora is very particular about her flowers."

I was just about to step in and try to smother the fire that was erupting when one clear voice spoke.

"I know why," John said.

Everyone became silent and looked toward him.

"It's because of me," John said quietly. "I found out a secret from her past, and I came here to try . . ." He trailed off and looked at the floor.

Doris, still boiling, turned her frustration toward him and boomed, "Tried what?"

He finally responded to his shoes, "To get money out of her."

A sharp gasp reverberated around the cottage, as if everyone were trying to suck the air out of the room. Lottie and Lavinia spoke the same words, at the same time, with very different emphases. "Oh God!"

He continued, "I was going to take her money, but then I met you all, and it didn't seem right. Doris always cooking me food. Annie knitting me sweaters. I had the evidence in a letter, but I lost it. The little round woman at the post office found it and put it through Flora's mail drop last night. I went everywhere this morning, just trying to find it before she saw it. Please believe me when I say I didn't want her to see it."

We all stood frozen as the truth of what he had said sank in.

Gracie broke the tension. She floated toward him and cupped his face with her delicate, childlike hands. Then she slowly raked her fingers through his hair, as if he were a young boy. "I believe you."

That one gentle act seemed to relax the group, and Lavinia spoke. "Well, what are we gonna do about it?"

"First things first," I said. "We need to tell Dan." I could tell by everyone's reaction that nobody was relishing that task.

Doris moved to the phone and picked it up. She called the local directory for the number of Dan's auto repair shop. I could hear the exchange clearly in the pin-drop silent gloom of the cottage.

"Hi, Doris," said the local operator. "How's your mama?"

"Mary, I don't have time to chat," Doris replied. "I have an emergency."

The operator went into business mode, and Doris wrote out the number she gave her and dialed. Two minutes later, Doris hung up the phone and looked at all our expectant faces. "Dan has gone out on a job. He'll be back in an hour. We'll call him back then."

"I don't know about the rest of you," said Lavinia, "but I need a quick something that's a little strong. I wonder if it's too early for a Baileys coffee at the Crab. We can't stay here. Besides, who knows? Maybe she just went for the night and will be back tomorrow. We shouldn't be too hasty."

Everyone agreed, but no one seemed convinced, I could tell. We filed out, locked Flora's door, and started toward the Crab.

Only John hung back. Lavinia noticed him and took him by the hand.

"Now, look," she said. "What's done is done. There's nothing you can do now. Everyone makes mistakes, and believe me, I'm the queen of them. I'm not sure how Dan will feel when he finds out, but you might as well get a cup of coffee to keep your strength up before he punches you on the nose."

John's face drained of color.

On the way to the Crab, he explained that it wasn't that he

hadn't been punched in the face before. He had—many times, he added. But somehow being in this quaint little Northwest town, with its flowering hanging baskets and "Southlea Bay Wants to Wish You a Happy Day" sign, had worn him down. It was hard for him to get back into his streetwise head. He no longer wanted —or seemed to remember how—to fight.

Lavinia nodded and smiled. "It's our one line of defense against meanness," she added. "All those dishes of pot pies and knitted gifts have a purpose."

As the group passed Ruby-Skye's shop, she poked her head out. "Going to a rally?"

"We're going to the Crab for breakfast again," said Gracie as she danced along on her toes in her bedroom slippers. "I love it when I get two breakfasts in one day."

I smiled and filled Ruby-Skye in quietly on the details.

"I'll be over in a minute," she said, going back into her shop to close it up.

Inside the Crab, the whole group gathered, waiting for our waitress, Gladys. When she saw us, she eyed John warily. "Who's this?"

"The booth," said Doris, ignoring her comment. "We need privacy."

"The booth?" responded Gladys, incredulously. "I can barely squeeze y'all in there, and now you have a man. What are you planning to do with him? Crush him in between you all or have him pop up out of a cake?"

John didn't look happy at either prospect.

"Maybe we could add a table," said Lottie thoughtfully.

Gladys grabbed a bunch of menus and shuffled off, complaining. "I should get my license to be a furniture mover just for when your gaggle comes in."

We followed obediently and squeezed as many of us into the booth as we could. Gladys tried to pull over a table, but as she pulled on it, nothing seemed to happen. She stood there with her hands stretched out on the edges of the table, puffing and panting.

John jumped in and moved the table for her, as if it were as light as a feather.

Gladys snarled again. "They don't pay me to be a weightlifter, you know."

We all sat down and Gracie squealed, "Look at all the people around this table. All we need is some ice cream and a cake with candles."

"Oh yes," said Lottie, playing along, "it's just like a birthday party."

"But without the hats and happiness," added Lavinia as she squinted at the menu. "Lottie, dear, do you have your reading glasses with you?"

Lottie shook her head, and Doris handed her a pair. "Oh, honey, those are too strong for me," she said, taking them off her face. "It all looks like it's written in Chinese."

I handed her mine, but they were too weak. "I feel like Goldilocks," she joked.

Gladys pulled out a smeared pair with a crack across them from her pocket, and Lavinia put them on.

"Gladys, these are just right, thank you." Lavinia looked ridiculous with the crack across the glasses and what appeared to be mayonnaise smeared across the corner.

Gladys, searching for a pencil in her bra, as usual, asked, "What is it to be, then?"

John looked terrified.

Once everyone had ordered and Gladys was gone, Doris beckoned us all in closer. "We need to think. If we were Flora, where would we go?"

"I just don't know" Lavinia furrowed her brow. "It's not like Flora to go off on her own like this. Why didn't she come to one of us?"

"Young man," said Doris sternly. "Exactly what did you write in that letter that scared her half to death?"

John stared down at his menu but didn't seem to be taking in much. He appeared to be preoccupied with his thoughts. Almost as if he were ashamed to put it into words.

Before he could say anything, Annie arrived at the table, a knitting bundle shoved under her arm. "I just heard from the lady in the bakery that Flora's gone missing. Is that right?"

"The bakery?" snapped Doris incredulously. "How did it whip around to there so fast? They're on the other end of town."

Gladys arrived back with the drink order, and Doris hushed everybody at the table.

Gladys raised her eyebrows and set down the drinks. "Though I appreciate you being as quiet as a church crowd," she said as she sniffed and pulled a bottle of ketchup from her apron pocket, "especially as some of you"—she glared at Doris—"can be more vocal than what's good for you . . ."

Doris flushed with anger but said nothing as Gladys brought out a tub of jam from the other apron pocket.

"But you should know," Gladys continued, "that if you're trying to hide it from me that the skinny, flighty one of your group took off in the middle of the night just before her wedding, I already know. My breakfast chef just told me."

She adjusted her apron and left.

Doris slammed her hand down on the table. "This town," she said. "I'd better call Dan before it hits the shoe shop. That's only across the road from where he works."

Doris dialed the number of the garage on her cell phone. She spoke with the owner for a second, then covered the mouthpiece before saying, "Dan has just walked in. I'm going to ask him to meet us here." She uncovered the mouthpiece and sounded as sweet as she could, which managed to sound odd coming from Doris—like an insane person trying to sound sane.

"Hi, Dan," she said, through her forced smile and glazed eyes.

"It's the Rejected ladies here. We have something we need to talk to you about. I wonder if you could meet us at the Crab. We're over here eating breakfast. Yes, it is sort of another surprise. You need to come straightaway, and don't stop to talk to anyone. OK, see you soon." Doris hung up.

"Maybe I should buy him a bottle of brandy," said Lavinia to her sister when she noticed Lottie's eyes were closed. "Oh Lord, she's already got her head down. By the way, her prayers are going up today. Who knows what they could bring in?"

John suddenly got up from the table. "I need to do something." He left the table and made his way to the back of the restaurant toward the bathrooms.

Gracie was making smiling faces on her pancakes with her syrup when Dan arrived at the table, his appearance grave as he approached us.

"Is it true?" he asked desperately. "Flora didn't turn up for her hair appointment? Her phone is off. I called her house phone again, but it just rang. I thought maybe she was with all of you." He looked frantically from face to face as he spoke, checking and rechecking for Flora's.

"How the blazes did you find out?" asked Doris.

"The guy who owns the gas station told me on the way to meet up with you all."

"You mean Derek? Now, how would he know?" Doris's tone was incredulous.

"It doesn't matter how he found out," I said, taking his hand. "Dan, I don't want you to worry. We're going to find her. She can't be far away. She doesn't even like to drive. She must have gone on a long walk or something. Please don't worry yourself."

"But she's taken her cat and the carrier," added Doris.

"Mr. Darcy never leaves Flora's home," added Gracie, sucking orange juice from her glass through a pink straw. "He likes being in her little cottage."

"Mr. Darcy is gone?" responded Dan desperately as he sank

down into a free chair. His face turned from distress to loss. He knew this was serious.

Just then, Gladys appeared at the table, pulled out her pencil, and shook her head.

"Oh, another man. You pack of cougars are in fine form today." Looking at Dan, she asked, "Will you be needing anything this morning? Soup is always a good choice for a broken heart. And don't worry, there're plenty more fish in the sea. You're not bad-looking. Not my type, of course," she added quickly. "But I'm sure there are lots of girls out there who wouldn't run off a few days before you walked them down the aisle."

The silence at the table was palpable. Only Gladys seemed oblivious to the atom bomb she had just dropped. She had Doris beat, hands down.

All at once, Ruby arrived and swooshed into the booth, wearing Indian pajamas and a satin turban.

"What did I miss?" she asked breathlessly.

Gladys answered her. "The fish is on, the wedding is off. The flighty girl ran off with her cat, and this fellow is on the market again if you're interested, though this lot already scared off the last red-blooded male they brought with them today." She finished her monologue dryly, with the signature greeting all the Crab waitresses generally sung out. "Have a Happily Dappily Day!" She put her pencil away, saying, "Nothing more, then? I'll be back with your bill."

Lavinia took Dan's hand. He looked so shocked. It was if he was weighing the truth in Gladys's words.

What if Flora didn't just have cold feet, I thought to myself, *but she actually didn't want to marry him? And left town to get away from him?*

Dan spoke before he appeared to realize it was audible. "Flora left me?" he said coldly.

The silence now broken, everyone started talking at once. I got up and sat down next to him. "No, Dan, you can't think like that. She lights up whenever she's around you. It's something more than that. Something's happened."

Dan looked frantic "What? What could have happened?"

Everyone became silent again as I tried to find the right words.

Unbelievably, it was Ethel who spoke. "It was that landscaping guy," she said, pointing at the spot where John had been sitting. "He blackmailed her."

Everyone now stared at the chair. He had left for the bathroom a long time ago, and it was obvious now he had no plans on coming back.

"What?" said Dan, his face changing from shock to anger.

"I'm afraid it's true," I said, trying to soothe him with my tone. "Apparently, John had some information about Flora—about Flora's past—but decided not to share it. He was going to destroy the evidence, but somehow she found out. We think that may be why she left."

The poor boy looked at me, heartbroken. He leaped to his feet and practically ran out the door, shouting over his shoulder, "I need to find her."

Doris slammed down her hand, making us all jump. "Cheryl Thompson," she shouted out jubilantly. She nodded at us, looking satisfied as she started to tuck into her sandwich. We stared at her as she added, "I just figured out how Derek found out about Flora. His wife's best friend is Cheryl Thompson, who does the garage's accounts for the woman at the Twinkle."

We spent the rest of our time at the Crab in emergency mode. Lavinia would cruise the town, Doris would get on the phone to everyone she could think of to call, I would be the point person collecting information, and Lottie would pray.

Dan called around midday to say that he'd asked everyone but no one had seen her. Also, the last-minute wedding jobs were stacking up, and he didn't know what to do about them.

I called Doris, who said, "I'm on it! I'll swing by Flora's now and pick up her wedding contact book and any information," and hung up.

Doris called an emergency meeting of the Rejected Writers' Book Club that evening at her house so we could all figure out the next step. All the ladies arrived worried and preoccupied, except Gracie, who stood in Ethel's place at the door, welcoming everybody to the house.

"Thank you all for coming again." She emphasized the word *again* as though she were offering a second ride on the carousel at the fair. The doorbell rang, and Dan arrived with Ethel in the front room. He'd aged ten years since that morning. He looked worried, pale, and antsy. The women smothered him in a hug as Gracie pinched his cheeks.

Lavinia was the first to speak from the love pack. "Dan, you have no idea how sorry we all are that this happened and that it was one of our own—John, our temporary group member—who was responsible."

"That's what you get for encouraging a man to be in our group," said Ethel from the bottom of the pack. She didn't appear to be hugging anyone but had somehow gotten gathered up as the ladies swooped in.

Doris banged her gavel. "Ladies, control yourselves. We have work to do."

Reluctantly, we retreated to our areas of the living room.

"Flora, wherever she is, is probably going to come to her senses before the wedding and realize she wants to be here, and when she does, we need to make sure there is a wedding for her to come to. So we'll split into two groups—the wedding planners and the searchers—and put our heads together to figure out where she might have gone."

CHAPTER TWELVE

TWIN CAT BURGLARS & A SHOCKING REVELATION

After the meeting, Lavinia and Lottie got into their silver-blue Cadillac and sat there for a minute.

"I can't believe this is happening," said Lottie with a sigh. "We have to think of all the ways we can help find poor Flora."

Lavinia started the car and rolled down Doris's driveway as Lottie stared out into the gloom.

She continued reminiscently, "It reminds me of the time when Hank threatened to kill you. Remember when we threw everything we owned into two suitcases and left in the middle of the night? Next thing we knew, we were on the road to who knows where."

"How can I forget?" said Lavinia. "Just like two cat burglars leaving the scene of the crime." As she thought of that night so long ago, an idea struck her. Lavinia spoke decisively. "We have to find out what was in that letter, Lottie dear. It's the key to this whole thing.

"I just remembered that when I got his letter, I was so scared that I didn't want to have it with me because I didn't want to take those hateful words, and it struck me that maybe Flora has done the same thing. If we can find out what made her run away, perhaps we can find out where she is."

"But John has disappeared, too," answered Lottie. "Doris tracked down where he was staying through our landscaper. He's embarrassed, no doubt. And we don't have the time or energy to track two of them. Flora's the most important."

"Maybe there is another way," said Lavinia, turning the Cadillac toward town. Ten minutes later they were back outside Flora's house, which was still shrouded in darkness. But Lavinia had an idea.

"What are we doing here?" asked Lottie.

"I have a hunch," said Lavinia, then she pulled out a flashlight from her glove box.

"Oh Lord," prayed Lottie as Lavinia jumped out of the car. "You know how my sister is when she gets like this. Keep us safe, for goodness sake."

Lottie joined her sister as Lavinia searched about the pots for the key. In the process, she managed to knock over Flora's garbage can, setting off the neighborhood dogs' barking.

"I can't find it," spat Lavinia in a hushed tone.

"Maybe Doris took it with her. We can go and ask."

"Why do that?" Lavinia's smile was devilish as she moved swiftly through Flora's side gate and into her back garden.

"Oh no," said Lottie, sending her eyes skyward as she trailed behind her sister.

Lavinia swung her beam about the garden, then set the light on what she was looking for in the corner—Flora's ladder. Lottie followed the beam and let out a breath.

"No!" she said before her sister had even spoken.

But it was too late. Lavinia was already making her way toward it. "Come on!" she said over her shoulder. "I noticed that the bathroom window was open this morning when we were in the house. I'll need help. Grab that end."

"I'm doing no such thing, Lavinia," Lottie said sharply. "This is ridiculous and I'll have no part of it."

Lavinia put a hand on her hip. "If we want to find Flora, we need to get into her house again. This morning we didn't look around because we didn't realize how important it might be in giving us clues."

Lottie stood rooted to her spot. Lavinia reached out to her imploringly as a last-ditch attempt. "Come on, Lottie. Flora needs our help, and we're running out of time."

But Lottie did not move.

Lavinia huffed at her sister's stubbornness. She pulled up the ladder leaning against the wall and tried to maneuver it all by herself around the garden. In the process, she knocked over some geraniums on Flora's patio, smashing a pot and setting off the dogs' barking again.

Lottie blew out air to illustrate her dissatisfaction. "Forgive me, Lord, for what I'm about to do." She begrudgingly grabbed the bottom of the ladder to help her sister maneuver it successfully across the garden. They pushed and pulled their way through a thick hedge, tiptoeing over the rest of Flora's potted plants.

Lavinia stated, out of breath, "Now then, that wasn't so hard, was it?" She placed the ladder against the back of the house and slipped off her green leather pumps. "Hold these, Lottie dear, will you?"

Lottie appeared worried, and by the movement of her lips, Lavinia knew she was already in full-on prayer mode.

Lavinia looked up and located the window.

So, apparently, did Lottie. "Lavinia," she said without even attempting to keep her voice down, "you can't mean that tiny, bitty thing? You're gonna try to climb in through that?"

"I'll be fine." Lavinia started to climb, leaving Lottie no choice but to hang on to the ladder to stop it from wobbling around.

"Lavinia Marie Labette," Lottie hissed in her big sister voice. "You will be the death of me."

"It's the opposite, you know. I'm what keeps your heart pumping," said Lavinia jovially. "Without my adventures, your heart would stop from sheer boredom."

Lottie, having moved from prayer to worry mode, said, "You're going to fall right off that ladder and break a hip, and then what will we do?"

Lavinia paused to think. "I suppose I'll have to go to the hospital to be cared for by one of those good-looking doctors."

"Lavinia!" hissed Lottie in a strained shriek.

Lavinia beamed down at her as she reached the top. She knew how to wind her sister up. At the window, she slipped her hand inside and was able to reach down and release the catch of the bigger window. Then, popping it off its latch, she sprang it open with such force, it crashed into the ladder and nearly knocked her off. She clung on as Lottie swore mildly.

"What did you say, Lottie dear?" inquired Lavinia, teasing her sister.

"You know exactly what I said," responded Lottie. "And now I have to ask forgiveness. I would say half of my forgiveness prayers come from something you've got me into."

Lavinia smiled and, having steadied her footing pushed open the window and pulled herself inside. Sliding gracefully to the bathroom floor, she poked her head out the window with the words, "Ta-da!" She placed her hands in the air, as if she'd just dismounted from the high bars at the Olympics.

Two minutes later, Lavinia had the door open for her sister.

"Piece of cake," said Lavinia triumphantly.

Lottie raised her eyebrows. "Now, why exactly are we here?"

"We have to try to find that letter."

"So you want us to search through her trash?" inquired Lottie indignantly.

"I do," answered Lavinia. "I bet the letter from John is still here."

Lottie sighed deeply. "Well, if we're going to be searching through trash, we're going to need some protection." She went to the kitchen and found flowery aprons and gloves for them both. She slipped one apron over her sister's head and handed her some gloves. They started in the kitchen and made their way to the bottom of the garbage, but nothing was there.

"Flora drinks a lot of peppermint tea," remarked Lottie as she heaped the trash back in. "That must be good for her."

They continued from room to room, rustling through the rest of the trash bins, but there was nothing. Lavinia looked despondent. "I was sure there'd be something. On all of those cop shows, they always find something interesting in the trash."

"What about the bedroom?" suggested Lottie, her eyes lighting up. "She may have opened her mail up there."

Lavinia smiled. "Let's check it out." She got up from her knees and made her way up the stairs, followed by her sister. They found a little basket under the side table and pulled it out. It was evident that Flora had opened wedding cards here, as a couple of them were on the side table and the envelopes were in the trash.

Lottie started reading through the cards. "'May your life together be blessed.' Oh, sister dear, oh my! I just hope this works out as it's meant to. Poor Dan, poor Flora."

Lavinia was only half listening as she fished through the basket. She pulled out a crumpled piece of paper and an envelope at the bottom. "Bingo!"

It was a letter. Underneath it, another large piece of paper had been stuffed back into an envelope.

She passed the letter to her sister. As Lottie tried to decipher the words, Lavinia pulled out the larger envelope and the piece of paper that was inside.

"Have you got your reading glasses, Lottie dear?"

"I have," she said, looking over the rim of them. "I'm using them to read."

"Well," her sister responded, "this looks more important." And before Lottie could refuse, Lavinia helped herself to her sister's glasses.

What she read made her sit down on the bed with a gasp.

"What is it?" Lottie said, trying to gauge her sister's reaction. "What does it say?"

Lavinia, for probably the first time in her life, was speechless. She handed the paper to Lottie, who removed the glasses from Lavinia's face and started to read. She only got halfway through before she sat down on the bed as well.

"This can't be right," she said, her throat tight with anxiety.

"Oh, it's right. I would know one of these anywhere. I have three of them, remember? This is a copy of a real wedding license. And if it's accurate . . ."

Lottie finished the sentence: "It means that Flora is already married to someone else."

Suddenly, there was a harsh knock at the door, and both women froze.

"Who could that be?" hissed Lottie.

"I don't know." Lavinia stuffed the letter and the photocopy into her pocket. She didn't want to leave it there for Dan to find.

Lottie hurried down the stairs, and from there she could see at least two looming shadows at the door, bright lights flashing in through the windows as someone banged again, and a gruff male voice shouted, "Open the door!"

Lavinia raced to the door, her heart pumping almost clean out of her chest. She unlocked it and was blinded by the flashlight. So was Lottie.

"Well, I can't see a damn thing," said Lavinia. "Put those blasted things out this minute!"

The flashlight beam swung toward the floor but, still suffering the ill effects of the light, neither sister could make out who it was, only a rough outline of what looked like two men: one squat and heavyset, the other tall and muscular.

Then a familiar voice: "I might have known it'd be you, Lavinia," said Sheriff Brown, Southlea Bay's law enforcement official. "When the people next door stated they'd seen two old ladies breaking into this house, I thought that didn't seem right. But now it all makes sense. Lavinia I can understand, but Lottie—how on earth did you get dragged into all of this?"

"Why, Sheriff, is that you?" Lavinia asked, shielding her eyes. She had always had a soft spot for men in uniform. "And is that your cute deputy with you?" she inquired, trying to focus on the sheriff's partner, a good-looking man with sandy hair and lovely blue eyes. "Why don't you come inside and keep us company?"

Lottie glared at her sister. The sheriff and his deputy moved into Flora's tiny sitting room and turned off the flashlights.

"I would offer you some coffee," said Lottie, "but I think Flora only drinks soy milk or something, and I wouldn't have the heart to put that in a working man's drink."

"What you should be offering me is an explanation," snapped the sheriff, folding himself down into one of Flora's little flowery chairs. He looked like an overstuffed teddy bear, a father playing house with his daughter. "Why the blazes are the pair of you climbing ladders and creeping around in the dark at this time of night, wearing aprons and rubber gloves?"

"Flora's gone missing," said Lavinia.

"I know. Dan came by the office earlier today to check if he needed to issue a missing person's report. But when a person leaves home a few days before her wedding, with her cat in tow, we don't generally tend to think the worst. It's been done before, and it will be done again."

"Officer, that doesn't sound like Flora—"

"Never mind all that. What are you two cat burglars doing creeping around in the middle of the night?"

"Well," said Lavinia as Lottie wrung her hands. Even from

across the room, Lavinia could hear her praying. "That's just the thing. Flora took off without telling any of us. We came by to see if there were any clues to let us know where she'd gone."

"You mean you were snooping," he said bluntly.

"Well, I suppose in a manner of speaking, we were—but with the best of intentions," added Lottie, slipping from her prayer for a second. "We are so worried about her."

"You can't break into someone's house no matter what your intentions are," responded the sheriff. "It's still a crime against Flora's privacy." He took off his hat and scratched his balding head before adding, "I should, by all accounts, arrest and charge you."

Lottie let out a cry.

But Lavinia, who had seen the inside of a jail cell, said, "Now, Sheriff, what would that accomplish? Flora's not even here to tell us whether it's a crime or not. We know exactly where her key usually is, but Doris Newberry must have walked off with it in her pocket. If she hadn't, we would have walked right in the front door. Think of all the paperwork, plus having to put us in a cell. What would that serve, really? And then Flora would come home and tell you she wasn't pressing charges because she knew our intentions were honorable. And isn't that all that matters—the intentions? Come on, Sheriff," Lavinia implored. "Let us lock up the house and go home. If you're really concerned, as soon as Flora gets back you can let her know you found us in here, and if she's not happy, you can have us arrested then. Maybe your other deputy would be on, and you wouldn't have to worry yourself about two old ladies who might have heart attacks from being in a cold jail cell all night." She finished her speech with a forced smile.

The sheriff exhaled and looked around the room. He seemed to be assessing if anything had been stolen, then appeared to resign himself to the fact this was probably going to be an open-

and-shut case. "Lavinia Labette, you give me a headache. For a lady in your sixties—"

Both women gasped as he mentioned their age.

The sheriff continued. "You give me more trouble than most teenagers. If there is a whiff of trouble in this town, it isn't long before it somehow gets connected back to you."

"I promise to be oh so good for a whole month," Lavinia assured him. Then she held up two fingers and added, "Scout's honor."

The sheriff let out a long, slow breath. "OK," he said, "just this once, Lavinia. But the minute Flora gets back, I will be down here explaining what happened, and if there's even a hint of wrongdoing, I'll be knocking on your door."

"Fine," said Lavinia. "That sounds like a deal. Now my sister can stop praying."

"Oh, is that what she's doing?" asked the deputy, who'd been searching the room while the sheriff talked to the ladies.

"She's all plugged into heaven," said Lavinia.

"It sounds like she's buzzing," he added.

"I know, like a little bee. But it keeps her happy," Lavinia added with a smile. Lottie looked irritated, but before she could say anything, Lavinia whispered, "Just keep quiet, honey, and we'll get out of this without a night in jail."

Lottie and Lavinia drove home in silence after they left Flora's, promising to keep out of trouble the rest of the month. But Flora's secret now weighed heavily on their shoulders.

CHAPTER THIRTEEN

TULLE TWIRLERS & BEACH REFUGEES

Doris was up early, and she had already called everyone she needed to in Flora's handmade *I'm Getting Married* book, which was decorated with doodled hearts and flowers. It looked a bit ridiculous in Doris's large, sensible hands as she turned the delicate pages. However, she'd managed to let everyone know that all the wedding details now needed to come exclusively through her.

She'd already fended off three calls this morning, and it wasn't even eight o'clock. The wine people needed to know where to deliver the wine (now that it wasn't Flora's house); the caterers wanted the Labettes' address for the tables and tablecloths delivery; and the man with the old-fashioned Buick, who'd been hired to chauffeur them away from the reception, wanted to know if he could switch out the car from a blue one to a green one. She'd read him the riot act, of course. "No bride wants to drive away in a green car," she said. "It plays havoc with her complexion and will make her look ill in the wedding photographs."

She'd just hung up the phone with him when it rang again. It was Carol Bickerstaff. She was frantic. All of Flora's flowers had arrived, and Flora was supposed to be there to help sort them.

"Don't worry," said Doris. "I will send someone down as soon as I have someone available. The Labettes are busy preparing the chapel, Annie has dogs arriving today for the Christmas holidays, and I already have a very long to-do list that seems to be getting longer by the second. But I'll figure something out."

~

I ARRIVED at Doris's door, a pile of tulle in one hand and Livvy in the other. I'd received a call to action an hour before: I'd been drafted into the wedding organizing committee.

Doris opened the door and sighed. "What's that?" she asked.

"The tulle for the flowers you told me to pick up for the gazebo," I said, bewildered.

"Not that," corrected Doris. "That." She pointed directly at Olivia.

"That is my grandchild!" I said defensively. "She's here to help me. Her mother needed to get some sleep, so Livvy is with me, and Grandpa has her brother, James. They're building a plane in the workshop."

Doris huffed and strolled back up the hallway as her three dogs bounded from the garden toward the open door and forced their way in.

Livvy clapped her hands. "Oooh, doggies!" she said and wriggled about in my arms. I put her down so she could pet them and followed Doris into the kitchen, which was already in full preparation mode: cellophane, ribbons, and more tulle in layers on every surface.

Gracie floated in behind me and squealed, "Oh, it looks just like we're having a wedding!"

Doris sighed. "We *are* having a wedding, Momma." Then she muttered to me, "She hasn't had her pills for two days. I have been so preoccupied with this wedding, I forgot to check her pill case. She's going to be terribly forgetful today."

Gracie pulled some tulle from the table and placed it over her head like a veil. "Who's getting married? I hope it's me. I would love to get married! I haven't slept with a man in a long time—at least, I don't think I have," she pondered, adding ribbon to her makeshift veil.

Ethel stopped filling little tulle bags with almonds and blinked twice.

"What can I do?" I asked.

"Take the tulle down to Stems and help Carol sort out the flowers. She's twice as busy handling the shop and the wedding flowers without Flora."

I pulled a face. "I'm not great with flower arranging."

"I'm fabulous," said Gracie, handing the tulle to Livvy, who automatically wrapped it around one of Doris's dogs.

"Yes, Momma is great. Why don't you take Momma with you to help?"

"Oh, OK," I said, chasing down a squealing toddler who was bounding after a dog in a tulle sash. "Any news from Dan?" Gracie followed after me as I hustled a wriggling toddler out the door.

Doris shook her head and waved us off.

~

WHEN WE ARRIVED at the flower shop, a very exasperated Mrs. Bickerstaff was hauling a delivery of potted plants inside, and every counter was covered with pink, cream, and mauve-colored flowers.

"Thank goodness!" she said.

"Looks like you're having a wedding," I said.

Mrs. Bickerstaff didn't appear to appreciate my joke and sighed deeply at the way the disheveled shop looked.

Gracie picked up the thought. "Yes, it does," she said. "Is someone getting married? I do hope it's me. I haven't been married in such a long time, I think." She wrinkled her brows and tried to remember. "I think I was married." She tugged at my sleeve. "Was I married?" she asked.

"Yes," I said, placing Livvy firmly on my hip while using my free arm to help Carol with the other end of a large potted plant.

"Who to?" asked Gracie.

"To Bill, for fifty years. Don't you remember, Gracie?"

"Oh yes," she giggled. "I remember him. He was a cute, strapping GI. He swept me right off my feet in my little town in England, where I lived. I was born there, did you know?"

"Yes, I knew," I said and then sighed as Livvy once again wriggled from my grasp to the floor. She raced away toward a display of I Love You bears that Stems often added to their flower deliveries. She grabbed one.

"Will I see him later?" asked Gracie.

"No, I'm afraid not," I answered. "He's gone, honey. He died."

"Oh," said Gracie. "That's right. I live with Dotty, now, so I guess it must be me that's getting married."

Mrs. Bickerstaff looked at me and Gracie and Livvy, who was now thoroughly enjoying herself, buried in the box of bears. Mrs. Bickerstaff's look seemed to say, *And this is supposed to help?*

An hour later, I'd wrestled some of the flowers into bunches. It had been a crazy, busy morning at Stems. Gracie slipped in and out of coherence. When she was with it, she was actually very helpful. But then this glazed look would cloud her face, and she would suddenly wander off to a section of the shop and start arranging something that was already arranged or cutting the bottom off flowers with a pair of scissors she'd managed to find till we took them off her. Once, she'd handed a loose bunch right to a customer who was leaving, saying, "Would you like fries with that?"

Livvy was no less stressful. She heaped every stuffed toy into the center of the shop and managed to break a bud vase in the process. As I finished adding ribbon to a little vase of violas on the counter, I looked across at Livvy and Gracie, who were twirling in layers of tulle. It was hard not to smile as the sunlight came in through the window and caught their tulle ballet. They were having such a marvelous time spinning in circles, the flimsy fabric draped around them like togas. They were giggling, and it was hard to see the difference between the adult or the child.

"It's so odd," said Mrs. Bickerstaff as she looked up from the arrangement she was putting together to watch them, "that at the end of our lives, we become like children again."

I smiled. It was true. They both seemed oblivious to the cares of the world, fully immersed, enjoying the moment. I envied them both.

Ten minutes later, done with twirling, Gracie approached the desk with Livvy, her accomplice, in hand.

"Dotty and I are going to the beach to collect shells," she said, the idea alive in her eager eyes.

"I'll need to come with you both." I answered.

"Wonderful," said Gracie, clapping her hands together. Before I could say another word, she'd already wandered out of the shop with Livvy in tow. I wiped my hands on my shirt as the florist's phone started to ring. Mrs. Bickerstaff picked it up.

"All Stems from Here," she said in her singsong greeting. She waved the receiver in my face and hissed, "It's for you. It's that Doris woman."

I glanced out of the window. There was a road between the shop and the beach, and I wasn't sure if Gracie remembered how to cross the street.

Mrs. Bickerstaff saw my concern and nodded at me. "I'll make sure the girls make it to the beach."

"OK," I mouthed back.

The miniature bell over the door tinkled as she left, just as a voice erupted from the receiver. "I need to ask you to bring in some little sprigs of fresh lily of the valley from the shop. I asked

Carol to order them especially for the table decorations. I'm going to be laying them out tonight."

"Great," I said, trying to finish the conversation quickly.

Mrs. Bickerstaff arrived back in the store, saying, "They're safely on their way. And don't worry, they're not in a rush. They're checking out a patch of daisies they found on the other side."

"Oh yes," Doris finally said. "A little lilac ribbon. Get that woman at the flower shop to cut four yards of lilac ribbon for the bunches of lilacs."

"OK," I said, trying to get off the phone.

"Oh, and there's something else."

I threw my eyes up in Mrs. Bickerstaff's direction as Doris paused for thought.

"Oh yes," said Doris. "How's Mama doing? She'll need to be back in about an hour to take her medication. I'm trying to get her back on track."

"She's fine, but I really need to go. She and Livvy are on the way to the beach."

"Is that wise?" inquired Doris as I started to break out in a sweat.

"Um, I was just thinking the same thing. I'd better go, bye."

I hung up before Doris could get another word in and hustled out of the shop. As I rushed down the street, I noticed it was a perfect winter day, one of those rare sunny days we sometimes get in December when the sun is shining and the temperature has warmed up a little. All about the village by the sea, Christmas was upon us. I noticed it as I made my way to the beach. There were threads of colored lights and wreaths of Christmas finery, and each shop was playing its own unique version of "We Wish You a Merry Christmas." The smell of coffee and cinnamon lingered heavy in the air.

As I approached the beach, the smell of saltwater was almost intoxicating. It took a minute for my eyes to adjust to the sunshine. I hustled onto the sand, searching frantically for Gracie and Livvy.

I saw the pair of them close to the water, both leaning over to peer at something on the sand. Livvy touched it, and even from the distance, I heard her shriek with delight. Gracie followed suit. It was amazing to watch the two of them together: Gracie with her candy-flossed white hair ruffled gently by the breeze next to Livvy's little soft locks, which were caught by the sunlight like a golden halo upon her head.

I relaxed a little. There was nothing to be worried about on the beach.

All at once, as if the gods wanted to prove me wrong, I caught sight of a golden retriever jumping through the frothy surf, barking and bouncing over the waves as they broke. Livvy spotted him immediately and started squealing, running toward the dog with great excitement. Gracie, a little slower, followed along on her tiptoes, her tiny birdlike voice reaching my ears across the wind: "Dotty dear, don't go . . . Dotty dear, come back." She skipped along after Livvy. I picked up my pace.

Suddenly, the dog turned and bounded toward its new playmate, barking and coaxing Livvy to play. Livvy obliged by racing straight toward the surf. I saw what was going to happen in slow motion.

A large wave.

A flash of movement.

Gracie arrived at Livvy's side just as a huge wave broke at their knees, knocking both of them off their feet.

I sprinted and reached them just as the wave receded back. They were giggling hard, completely drenched from head to foot.

I raced straight for Livvy and picked her up as the retriever bounced up to greet me, too. He was overexcited, and I was already off balance. As I stretched forward to help Gracie up, he pounced, and his wet, sandy paws caught me in the small of my back. I went down, too, and we all collapsed in a mangled wet sandy heap. I felt my weak wrist, the one I had injured on our road trip, give way beneath me.

Livvy squealed again as the dog used the opportunity to cover us all in wet doggy kisses. His owner arrived to help, giving us her apologies while explaining he was still a puppy.

"So are these two," I said wryly as we all managed to get to our feet. I looked down at the three of us. In the space of two minutes, we'd gone from clean to a soggy, freezing, sandy mess. I squelched to the shore, and my arm ached terribly.

We arrived at Doris's fifteen minutes later. Ethel opened the door and looked me up and down. She started to shut the door on me when Doris shouted from the kitchen, "Who is it, Ethel?"

"That homeless woman you took pity on went out and got everyone dirty. That's who it is. And if I were you, I wouldn't let them drip all over your carpet."

Doris arrived at the door, pink sugar icing decorating her hair, face, and apron. We were all huddled in a blanket I kept in the car, three refugees hoping she would take pity on us.

Doris eyed us critically as Gracie's face lit up. "We all went to the beach and had so much fun!"

Doris shook her head. "Get some newspaper, Ethel. We'll have them brush off as much as we can out here, and then we can drop their clothes onto the newspaper."

"It was an accident," I said, avoiding Doris's admonishing gaze. "They ended up on the beach, and a dog knocked them into the water."

As if on cue, one of Doris's own dogs arrived at the door and pushed past us. Livvy, who was already balanced precariously on my hip, slipped to the floor, shouting, "Doggie!" and chased him through the house, almost knocking Ethel from her feet as she placed newspaper sheets on the floor. Livvy sprayed clumps of sand and water everywhere as she went. I ran after her, realizing halfway down the hall that she still had on her sandy shoes, and so did I. I slipped mine off and finally caught up with her, but it was too late. She had caused the most amount of damage a child could do in two minutes flat.

Carrying the wriggling toddler, I arrived back at the door. Gracie was twirling on the paper and had taken off her clothes, right down to her slip. She asked me, "Are we going dancing?"

I hung my head desperately.

Thirty minutes later, a newly washed Livvy and I emerged into the kitchen after taking a shower in Doris's bathroom. The room was now a hive of activity. Gracie was high on a stool, mixing a batch of cake batter, and when I came in, she said to Livvy, "I'm making dish cakes!"

"You mean cupcakes," replied Doris.

"You can help, if you like," added Gracie.

About thirty minutes later and with sprinkles everywhere—even down my bra—I felt exhaustion taking over. "I'm going to take Livvy home," I said. "I only have one more diaper, as she managed to get the last one soaking wet."

Doris nodded. "Call me later. I'll see where we are with the preparations."

When I got home, my aching arm had started to swell quite badly, but there were still the twins to deal with. So I iced it the best I could. When Martin arrived home after having to go into work for a few hours, he found a frosted-faced Livvy curled up on her grandmother's lap and an eggy-faced James lying across his mother. The children and Stacy were all out cold. He looked around the house. It was as if someone had been through it with a hurricane. I waved meekly at him.

"The front door was open," he whispered.

I shrugged.

I watched him as he surveyed the scene. There was a trail of dry cat food all the way up the hall. The rest of the packet had been tipped into the cat water and was floating in there like little brown-and-orange fish. A whole roll of bathroom tissue had been creatively wound around the banister. In the front room, the TV was blaring children's programs, and every cushion we weren't sitting on had been taken off the sofa. He walked straight back out the front door and returned twenty minutes later with Chinese food. Stacy opened one eye. "Hey, Dad," she said as she rubbed her eyes.

"Looks like you guys had fun," he said as he rewound the toilet paper.

"Doris gave us too much sugar," I stated. "Livvy was making cupcakes."

"Making or eating?" inquired Martin, noticing Livvy's pink buttercream mustache.

Martin kissed Stacy and me on the head. Taking Livvy from me, he carefully laid her on the sofa and then did the same with James. As I got up, I winced with pain. He looked down at me, and I looked down at my hand, which had doubled in size. "What did you do to your arm?" he asked.

"I fell on the beach. I don't fall well."

"The beach?" he asked quizzically. "You should probably have it checked out," he added with concern as he dished up Chinese food for us all. We sat at the breakfast bar, eating, enjoying the rare moment of quiet. It was just after we finished that James came running in from the living room, his eggy face smiling and his trousers obviously wet, his last diaper not holding out.

"I should get the twins in the bath," Stacy said.

I reached toward James to help her, and I winced again.

"OK, Grandma," said Martin, taking James from me. "I'm going to help Stacy with these babies and bath time, and we're going to the hospital as soon as I'm finished."

I started to object, but Martin shook his head.

"Just to be on the safe side," he said. "Besides, I can't remember the last time I got to play in the bath with the kids." He smiled as Livvy arrived from her nap and kissed him on the nose. "See how cute they are? How come we didn't have more?" he asked, smiling.

I panned the room with my hand.

Stacy moved toward the bathroom, and I hugged her.

"What was that for?" she asked.

"Because I'm so proud of you. You're an amazing mother, and you're doing such a great job."

Tears sprang to Stacy's eyes. "Thank you, Mom. I had a good role model." Then, as if she'd been too vulnerable, she looked at the floor. "I'd better get them in the bath. Are you sure you're OK?" she asked, looking at my arm.

I nodded and shooed her toward the bathroom.

After she left the room, I heard James squeal with delight, and then something crashed to the floor, and our cat, Raccoon, bolted out of the bathroom and disappeared. *Oh, the joys of raising small children,* I thought. I'd forgotten how bone tiring it was. I sipped a glass of wine Martin had poured for me and grinned through my pain. This was family in all of its glory.

An hour later, with two scrubbed-cheeked angels lying in bed together while Stacy read them a book, Martin and I slipped off to the hospital. I looked down at my arm. It didn't seem to be going down at all.

"Do you hear that?" asked Martin as we headed off into the dark, cold night.

"What?" I said. "I can't hear anything."

"Exactly," he said. "Isn't it amazing?"

"They sure are a lot of noise and energy, but I think they've been good for Stacy. She actually told me tonight she thought I'd been a good mother."

Martin looked at me with his eyebrows raised. "Wow! Who knew what eighteen months of no sleep could do?"

An hour later, I was seated on the plastic examining table at the doctor's, who stared at my X-rays, which he had put up on the light box next to him. Martin was fascinated by all the technology.

"You have a hairline fracture right across your radial" said the doctor. "We should probably set it, give it a chance to heal itself."

Martin pointed to the X-ray. "Is that here? Is that it?" he asked, like a kid finding the right puzzle piece of a jigsaw.

The doctor nodded and went into full-explanation mode on how the bones in the arms work together. I coughed after about ten minutes of Bone Fractures 101.

"OK," said the doctor, "let's get this set and get you home."

We finally arrived home about half past eleven, and I found Stacy actually sitting alert on the sofa, looking through one of our old photo albums. Martin, tired from driving, excused himself.

"Oh no," said Stacy, noticing my arm. "I'm so sorry, Mom."

Yes, this is a very different Stacy, I thought. She never used to be able to see anyone else's pain but her own.

"Oh, I'm fine," I said. "It's just a hairline fracture, but I'll have to keep this on for about six weeks. I can't believe I'm wearing another cast—the second in just a couple of years." Before that, I'd never even had a tooth out. "I thought you'd be in bed, darling." I sat down and poured myself another glass of wine.

"No," she said, "I like to have just five minutes to think without the twins late at night. Sometimes that is the only time for myself."

I paused. I thought this might be the best time to bring it up. "What's going on, Stacy?"

Stacy looked up, confused.

"You and Chris?" I added.

The pain on Stacy's face was obvious. She tried to find the right words. "It's all my fault."

Was she just admitting responsibility? That was growth, for sure.

"I've been so resentful because he still gets to go to work and I have to stay home, which in one way I love and another, I hate. My loss of my individuality, all my single friends, all the things that made me who I am have gone. I've been pushing him away for months, and finally, last week, he left."

Stacy started to cry, large tears sliding down her face. I looked for the right words.

"Having babies is a major change for anyone," I said. "Having two is like a double stress. Is there any way you think you could work it out?"

"I have no idea," she said. "I'm not sure how he feels right now. I haven't spoken to him for a week. He's tried to call, but I just haven't had the heart to pick it up or call him back." She sniffed, saying hurriedly, "I need to go to bed."

This was her way of closing down. She'd never been good at exposing her underbelly. She downed the last of her wine, kissed me on the head, and exited, saying over her shoulder, "Better get some sleep, Mom. We've got the same thing all over again, tomorrow."

I sipped my wine and looked at the photo album Stacy had abandoned. I probably hadn't opened it in over five years—not since we had come to Southlea Bay. I smiled as I looked at all the pictures of young Stacy growing up, and it stung me to see her with both a mom and a dad. I wanted that for her children. I shut the book and went upstairs. Martin was snoring softly. I hesitated but made a decision.

"Martin," I whispered as I shook him gently. He was dead to the world, so I shook a little harder. "Martin," I said. He turned over, looking discombobulated. "Are you OK? Do you need something for your arm?"

"No, I'm fine," I said. "I've had a couple of painkillers, and now that it's in a cast, it feels much better."

"Well," he said, "what is it?"

"I've been thinking we should invite Chris up for a couple of days. He and Stacy could have a mini vacation, just the two of them."

Martin rubbed his face, trying to understand what I was

saying. "And have us look after the two holy terrors, Poopy and Dribble?"

I smiled and raised my eyebrows.

"Oh no," he said. "I'm not sure I could do a whole two days."

"Do you know what those children need?"

"Jail?" he offered sarcastically.

"A father and a mother," I responded dryly. "That's the best thing we can make happen, even if it means taking care of them for one weekend so their parents can reconnect. I'm willing to sacrifice a couple of days."

Martin sighed. How could he argue with that?

"What makes you think he'll come up here?" he asked, obviously hoping for another way out.

"I know he loves Stacy, and I know she loves him. We just need to give them some time where their whole emotional space is not taken up with those two little spitfires. I need you to be on board because I can't drive anywhere at the moment," I said, flashing my cast.

As if to punctuate our conversation, James started to cry and shout out in his sleep, "Daddy, I want my daddy."

Martin looked up at me. "How did you pull that one off?"

"It's meant to be." I said, raising my eyebrows in an all-knowing fashion.

"OK," he said. "When are you planning this fabulous vacation for us?"

"I'm going to call Chris in the morning," I said, trying to undress with one arm.

He watched for a second, enjoying the crazy show before he finally got out of bed, lifted my nightgown over my head, and kissed me on the cheek, saying, "As I always say, things are never boring around here with you."

CHAPTER FOURTEEN

A BLUE CADILLAC & A CAR FOR CLOWNS

The Labette sisters both had another sleepless night. They tossed and turned, and when "Angels We Have Heard on High" rang out through the house at five thirty in the morning, both of them bolted upright in their beds.

The sisters met each other on the landing in their night attire. Lottie reached out to Lavinia, saying one word: "Flora."

"Robes," responded Lavinia as they raced to their combined closet.

They put on their slippers. Lavinia grabbed a pink robe, and Lottie the pale-blue one.

"I like the pink," Lavinia said. "It's friendlier."

"Flora loves pink, but I'm already in blue," said Lottie.

"But the pink looks better," said Lavinia.

The angels chimed away again.

"Hell, who cares about the robes? We need to go down and let that poor girl in."

Lavinia raced down the stairs and pressed the "Open" button on the gate keypad without even looking to see who it was, but when she opened the door, it wasn't Flora.

"It's Dan," Lavinia said as Lottie joined her at the doorway, now wearing the pink robe.

"Did you find her?" they asked in unison.

"No," he said. "But I think I know where she's gone."

Lavinia pulled him inside, and they all moved into the kitchen. He was animated; he started to pace. He was unshaven, and he looked like he was wearing the clothes from two days before. He spoke in a long, jumbled monologue. "I kept trying to recall if she had mentioned a relative or a friend, but you know Flora's whole life revolves around Southlea Bay. She only ever left once, when she went to Canada to study art for college one summer. Apart from that, she's always been here, especially since her parents died. I know she has some distant relatives on the East Coast, but she hardly knows them, and I can't see her getting on a plane with Mr. Darcy and flying to New York City."

Lottie shivered with the morning chill as he continued to speak.

"Then, in the middle of the night, I suddenly remembered she'd told me about a place in Leavenworth. A place she went with her family. A place where she felt safe and visited after her mother and father died. I Googled the name of the cabin but nothing came up, and her phone seems to be off. I'm pretty sure that's where she is, and I can't just sit around here. So I was wondering—as you ladies know her so well, and the rejection group is the closest she has to a family—whether you would be available to come with me?"

Lottie lifted her hands and her face glowed. "God has answered my prayers," she said. "I'll put on some coffee so we can discuss the very idea."

"So we can plan the rescue," Lavinia added.

Lavinia and Dan moved into the living room, but Dan found it hard to settle. He was antsy as he paced around the room. He was describing the place in Leavenworth to Lavinia when Lottie arrived with a cup of coffee and put it in his hands. "You're freezing," she said to him.

He gulped down a mouthful. "The only thing I wish I knew was what made her do it. Why didn't she talk to me about whatever it was that was bothering her?"

Lavinia and Lottie exchanged a brief glance but Dan didn't catch it.

Deep in thought, he continued, "I have to admit, I had a bad feeling about John. I went over last night to the place where he stays, but they said he took off with all his stuff that afternoon, and no one has seen him since. Probably a good thing, I'm not sure what I'd have done if I'd found him."

Dan flexed his fist, and Lottie tapped him on the shoulder. "John will get what's coming to him. Mark my words: *what goes around comes around.* I actually think he was gut wrenched that Flora got a hold of that information. I truly believe he was going to destroy the letter before she received it, so he isn't all bad. We think he came here with an evil intent, but we all won him over with our fabulous small-town charm." Her eyes sparkled.

"I want to get going as soon as possible," Dan said. "That's why I'm here. It's going to take about three or four hours to get up to Leavenworth. We have no time to lose. I'm not sure what I did to upset her, but I want her to have a friend when I get there, and maybe I'm not it . . ." His voice trailed off, and he looked down at his hands.

Lavinia took hold of one of them and squeezed it tightly. "We'll be ready in a jiffy. Taking off in the middle of the night is my and Lottie's specialty."

"Why don't you go and get the car gassed up, and pick us up at six o'clock?" Lottie suggested.

"Oh Lord, is it only five thirty?" said Lavinia.

"I hope no one from my church sees me," Lottie said. "It will look bad, me leaving town with a young man at six in the morning."

"Not for me," said Lavinia with a wry smile. "People wouldn't expect anything less."

Her eyes twinkled as she let Dan out the door, and the ladies made their way up the stairs to get ready. Pulling out their overnight cases, they started packing their clothing.

"Something warm," said Lavinia.

"Then we'll need those blue boots," added Lottie.

"Lottie," said Lavinia.

Lottie continued to pack the pink raincoats. "I know what you're going to say. Black pumps." Lottie hovered in front of her case. "I think we should tell him something before he sees Flora, about the letter. Otherwise, he may want to turn around and not go after her. He may just be too heartbroken."

"But he may not want to go at all, then," stressed Lavinia as she tossed some pantyhose into her suitcase. "We have to give Flora a chance to put this right."

"Violet blouses," mumbled Lottie as Lavinia headed for her underwear drawer.

Lottie slammed her hands down on her case with frustration. "I still can't believe it. Flora married! She's as quiet as a church mouse and barely leaves the island. What if the whole thing is a mistake, or even a forgery?"

Her attention in her underwear drawer, Lavinia furrowed her brows. "If it's a forgery, why did Flora take off? There has to be some truth in it. Otherwise we'd be hearing about it at one of our Rejected group meetings, in one of her 'I wonder what's happened to all the good in the world' poems."

"Good point," said Lottie, adding, "Red skirt."

"We don't own a red skirt."

"I mean shirt," said Lottie, preoccupied.

Suddenly, their phone rang. Lottie headed down the stairs to pick it up, saying, "It isn't even five forty-five and we have people calling and knocking down the door."

She didn't allow her irritation to creep into her voice when she picked up the receiver. It was Ruby.

"I was ringing my Tibetan singing bowls on the beach, and my inner goddess told me to give you a call."

"Yes, we're going to Leavenworth. Dan thinks Flora might be there. I'll call Dan and tell him to pick you up if you like." Then Lottie had a thought. "Ruby?"

"Yes?"

"What're you wearing right now?"

"My birthday suit," she said and chuckled. "You know I hate wearing clothes when I'm meditating."

"But it's freezing out there," Lottie shrieked back.

"Bracing," corrected Ruby.

"Well, I think it might be appropriate to put something on before that young man gets there. He doesn't need any more shocks this week."

"Oh, OK, Mom" she said in a singsong tone. "I'll throw something on. Namaste."

"Ham and what?" inquired Lottie into the silent receiver. Realizing Ruby had gone, she muttered, "Bless her heart" absently as she hung up the phone.

When Dan returned, both the twins stood in the driveway with their little suitcases at their feet. In the car was Ruby, now dressed in a snow suit. Dan jumped out, asking, "Are you ready?"

Lavinia looked at the tiny car and said, "I hope you don't think we're all going to travel in that bumper car. We're not clowns, you know."

Dan looked at his little Honda like he hadn't even thought about what it would take to get them all in.

"We also have to pick up Annie on the way. She wants to come. She came along for the cross-country craziness we went on, and she and Flora became very close. She thinks she might be able to help that poor girl see some reason. I called Janet, too, but she has grandbabies right now, so her brain's all Jell-O, though she said she might try to drive down herself and meet us there."

"Well, if we don't take my car, what do you suggest?" asked Dan.

"The Cadillac, of course," said Lottie, as if that was her plan from the beginning. "We always keep the tank full, and that old car likes a nice little journey now and again. We'll enjoy the wind in our hair."

"Even though it's like thirty degrees," added Lavinia. "Annie's still getting hot flashes. She'll probably need the top down to keep her cool."

Dan seemed bemused by all this female information, looking especially tired after what Lavinia surmised was two nights of no sleep.

"OK," said Dan, apparently anxious to get on the road.

"She's in the garage. Would you be a dear and pull her out into the driveway for us?" said Lavinia, flashing a warm smile and batting her eyelashes.

Ten minutes later, they were all loaded into the twins' blue Cadillac. It was clean as a whistle, and the cream upholstery was shiny, the chrome newly polished.

"We only had it detailed last week," said Lottie as they all climbed in. "May as well travel in comfort. Now, let's pick up Annie on the way and get going."

Dan pulled out of the twins' driveway as Lavinia, who had commandeered the front seat, brushed his hand with hers, saying, "Don't worry, Dan. We're going to find your bride and bring her back. You're going to have the perfect wedding, and Flora is going to get married."

Lavinia then turned her head back and couldn't resist adding the word *"again"* in a whisper to her sister, who tapped her shoulder and mouthed *"Lavinia!"* in a silent outcry.

Ruby pulled out a CD from her little Ban the Bomb bag and handed it to Dan. "Here," she said. "For the journey."

He pushed it into the CD player and the song "Turn! Turn! Turn!" filled the car. They all couldn't help but join in the chorus —all except Dan, whose eyes and thoughts were fixed on the road.

As they pulled into Annie's farm, and Dan slowed the car to a stop barking escalated. Annie had kept kennels for many years and didn't even seem to hear it anymore as they all shouted their greetings. Already packed, she jumped into the car, and they made their way to catch the seven a.m. ferry.

They arrived just in time.

"This is great. We'll be there by ten," commented Dan as he parked the Cadillac on the ferry. They had twenty minutes before they arrived at the other side.

"I think I need a cup of coffee and some air to keep me awake," said Lavinia. "Do any of you want anything?"

They all shook their heads as Lavinia got out of the car and made her way up the stairs to the upper deck.

CHAPTER FIFTEEN

FERRY FORAYS & MOMENTS OF TRUTH

John sped down the hill and just managed to slide into the last space on the early-morning ferry. He shut off the engine and hunched over the steering wheel of his Pinto, which he'd slept in overnight. He had finally gotten the money from a friend to get him off the island. He was tired and cold and ready to get out of this place . . . or was he? He felt a knot in the pit of his stomach. Every time he thought of Flora, he felt this churning guilt. These people had been nothing but kind to him, and he'd repaid them by ruining Flora's wedding.

He pushed his hand deep into his pocket and located his cigarette box—it was empty. He looked around until he spotted a set of stairs and wondered if there was somewhere to get cigarettes up there. He managed to disentangle himself from his car and stand up, feeling stiff and tired.

He scanned the cars around him; this seemed to be a commuter ferry. The majority of the people appeared to be going to work. Everyone looked like they were from somewhere and had a place to be. He not only didn't fit—he had no place to be. No one cared if he lived or died. He used to like that about his life; it made him feel free as a bird. Now seeing all these travelers made him feel lost somehow. He hated that. He pulled his jacket close around his neck, shoved his hands deep into his pockets, and made his way up the stairs. He headed to the coffee counter and bumped into someone who was turning with a cup in her hand.

"John!" she exclaimed. It was Lavinia.

He looked frantically around for a place to escape to, but the coffee counter was packed and he was blocked in at every turn.

"What are you doing here?" she asked. "We've been looking for you everywhere." The concern in her voice disarmed him for a minute. So there had been no posse to run him out of town on a rail? He was sure if he saw anyone again, he would've gotten punched in the nose.

"Ms. Lavinia," he said, "I have to go."

"We're on a twenty-minute ferry trip. There is nowhere for you to go. I need to speak to you right now. You ran off before anyone could straighten this thing out."

For a minute, John had a glimmer of hope. "Did Flora come back?"

"Why don't you take my cup of coffee, and you and I can go and have a little talk about that?" she said, smiling.

John felt trapped. He hadn't expected to see any island people again, and here he was, face-to-face with one of the very people he was trying to escape. Lavinia found a table and sat down. "Stop looking at me like that," she commented. "I ain't the principal of the high school. This is me—Lavinia. There isn't one thing you've thought up that I haven't done. I know exactly how you feel right now, believe me."

He looked down at the table, hanging his head. "You don't understand. I did a terrible thing to Flora."

Lavinia smiled. "You mean sending her a letter with her wedding certificate in it?"

He looked up, shocked.

"Lottie and I found it. But don't worry, no one knows about it but us. Now, we're going to start at the beginning, and you're going to tell me the whole story."

John could see he wasn't going to get away with not telling her everything. She had a persuasive air—and besides, he liked the old girl. She'd obviously lived in her day, and she had always been nice to him. He swallowed deeply and realized he wanted a cigarette, powerfully, with all his might, but that would have to wait. "It's a long story," he said.

"Why, I have the whole ferry ride!" said Lavinia, batting her eyelashes.

"Two years ago, I met a guy named Andy. He was a graphic artist, and he needed someone to help him with an extension. Andy and I hit it off, and we started hanging out together. One night, we went out drinking, and he talked about how he was considering proposing to his girlfriend. And then he joked about how it wouldn't be like the last marriage. Apparently, he'd had a great opportunity to go and work in the States, and he talked this girl, Flora, into marrying him for a green card. She had been getting an art degree up there. He had the idea that if he married an American citizen, all his troubles could be over."

"That sounds like something Flora would do. She is a little naive and helpful to a fault."

"Anyway, they got married. Everything went according to plan, or so they thought. But getting the annulment didn't turn out as easy as he'd thought. He didn't have the heart to let Flora know since she'd been so kind to him. So he lied to her and told her the annulment had taken place and everything would be fine, thinking he'd figure it out after she had gone.

"Fast forward a few years, and here I was with Andy, who was on the verge of proposing to this girl, and he'd lost touch with Flora. All he remembered about her was she lived on an island somewhere in the Pacific Northwest. He managed to finalize the divorce a few months ago and wanted to get the paperwork to her. And I offered to do that for him—for a price, of course."

"Of course," said Lavinia tartly.

"That's when I saw dollar signs. If she didn't have the paperwork, I could lead her on, telling her she was still married and offer a price to solve her problem, pretend I was going to serve the papers to Andy, get paid both ways. I thought she might have a life here, a boyfriend, or a wealthy family, someone I could leverage for some money."

Lavinia sipped her coffee as he continued.

"She was hard to track down, but eventually I found an article in the *Bay Breeze* about a show she was in last year to raise money. But when I got here and found out she was actually in the process of getting married, that meant I had even more power. That's when the whole plan backfired. I was going to give her the official final divorce paperwork the morning she disappeared—I swear—then I found out the original letter I wrote, demanding money and telling her she was still married, had gone missing."

Lavinia nodded. "That's some story, but all that matters"—she took his hand—"is that you really did plan to do the right thing. Do you still have the documents that prove her divorce is final?"

"Yes," he said and nodded. "In the car."

"Why don't you come with us to Leavenworth? You can tell Flora yourself how sorry you are. Things could still be saved so she knows it's OK to marry Dan."

John shook his head. "I'm bad luck. There's no place for me in this."

Lavinia cocked an eyebrow "Honey, believe me, there is always hope."

An announcement came over the speakers, telling the passengers they would be arriving at the dock shortly and they should return to their cars.

John jumped to his feet. "I need to get back on the road. Let me give you the papers, and maybe if you find Flora, she'll have a wedding after all."

Lavinia followed him quietly to his car, and he handed her a large manila envelope. She took it and looked at him. "Are you sure you don't want to give it to her yourself? I think it would do you a lot of good to find forgiveness."

For a moment, it looked as if John was considering it. Then he took a deep breath, pulling his jacket up around his ears. Giving her a half smile, he got into the car, adding, "You're not as bad to the bone as you make out, Ms. Lavinia."

Lavinia smiled and took it as a compliment. She put the large envelope in her purse and signaled to him to lower his window.

"Good-bye, John. We'll miss you." When she gently kissed him on the cheek, he seemed visibly shocked by it, and Lavinia couldn't help saying as she walked off, "Those kisses don't come cheap, so make sure you savor that one."

∼

SHE ARRIVED BACK at the car just as the ferry bumped gently into its mooring. Lottie was wringing her hands, beside herself.

"My goodness, Lavinia, where on earth have you been? We've been getting really worried."

Lavinia slipped into the passenger seat of the Cadillac and pulled down the mirror, cool as ice. She pulled out her lipstick and gracefully reapplied a coat. Then she said quietly, after pushing her lips together to coat them evenly, "I got myself some nice fresh air."

∼

THE NEXT MORNING, I was up early. I hadn't slept well. The painkillers had done their job well enough, but sleeping in the cast had been uncomfortable. It woke me up several times in the night. I sneaked into Stacy's room. Both twins had left their beds and were draped over her in one fashion or another. James had his foot in her face, and Livvy was lying across the pillow, trapping Stacy by the hair. I grabbed her phone to take a picture, but I didn't want to risk the chance of waking any of them, so I crept down to the kitchen to try to figure out Stacy's phone. I pulled up the message tab by mistake and found lots of messages from Chris. He sounded sad and confused. To me, it just confirmed that I was doing the right thing.

I located Chris's number and walked out on the deck, huddling in my heavy robe and slippers. It was a lovely, fresh morning, and the squirrels leaped around in the grass, looking for any traces of food. I smiled as I dialed the number.

He picked it up on the second ring. "Stace," he said. The desperation and relief was obvious.

I felt a pang and hoped that I was still doing the right thing.

"No, Chris, it's me, Janet," I said.

"Oh," he said, disappointed. Then, as an afterthought: "Is everything OK? Are the twins OK?"

"Yes," I said. "They're having a marvelous time up here with us. They seem to be changing by the day." I automatically regretted saying that, knowing how sad he would feel to be missing out on their lives. "Look, I'm going to get straight to the point. I think you need to come up here and spend some time on the island. I think you and Stacy need some quality time together. You two belong together, and for the sake of the babies, you should at least give it a try."

There was a long silence on the other end and I wasn't sure if he'd hung up. Then he spoke. "Does Stacy know you're calling me?"

For a second there, I heard hope in his voice. I didn't want to take that hope from him, but I needed to be honest. "No, she doesn't, Chris. But you and I know this can't be the end of the story. Raising children can be very hard, and there's a lot of work. Raising two at the same time and the same age is very hard, indeed. It's going to take both a mommy and a daddy to do it. Please, I think it would be a good thing if you and Stacy just took some time away from work and your own pressures at home."

He was quiet again. I could hear the static on the line and the traffic noises around him as I nervously waited for his decision. Then he said, "I'm on my way to work right now. Let me talk to my boss and see if I can get a few days off. Maybe you're right."

"You know I'm right."

"OK," said Chris. "I will call you in a little while."

About half an hour later, Chris called and told me he had booked himself on the next flight out of San Francisco, and he would be there around midday. "I'll send Martin out to pick you up," I said cheerfully.

Martin was just kissing me *good-bye* on the head as he heard that comment. He had on his overcoat, and his briefcase was in his hand. He picked up a sandwich I had made for him and said, "Martin will pick whom up, when?"

"Chris from the airport," I stated as I hung up the phone, trying to sound matter-of-fact.

His eyebrows disappeared into his hairline. "Then I might need to pick up a bottle of scotch, too," he joked as he walked toward the door. "I hope you know what you're doing, Ms. Matchmaker."

"Of course," I said, pushing him out the door and watching him walk to the car. But once back inside, I was having second thoughts. What if Chris's coming here made things worse? What if Stacy felt betrayed by me when we'd really just started to bond? I nearly ran back to the phone and called him back, but something in my gut told me this was going to be OK. I just had to trust it.

Stacy appeared behind me.

"Hello, honey," I said. "How did the twins sleep?"

"Not bad," she said. "They got five hours, which is decadent for me."

I went into the kitchen to make Stacy and myself a cup of tea.

As I boiled water in the kettle, Stacy said, "You know, you and Dad have been great. It makes such a difference being here and having your help. It can be so hard on your own."

I wondered for a moment if should I tell her about my plans, but instead I decided to enjoy this moment with my daughter. She really was becoming a lovely person to be around.

"I think being an only child wasn't always a good thing for me," she continued as she yawned and pulled herself up on a stool at the kitchen island, hugging her cup of hot tea with her hands. "I think that in some ways, I was a little brattish. Having the twins sure sorted that out. I never have a moment to think about myself. I know I've been resentful at times about what they need. I feel so guilty because so many people can't have children or they have sick kids, and I'm so blessed. But I have to tell you, Mom, I thought labor was hard, but trying to do this day after day, without dropping down from exhaustion, is the hardest thing I've ever done."

I thought I would gently push the needle in the right direction. "I know what you mean. Having your dad around was a great help when you were younger. He helped share the load a lot."

"Yes," she said. "I know it would be a little easier if Chris was around, but I've been thinking about what you said the other day, and I think things are too far gone for either of us to make our way back down that road."

"Maybe if you had some time together alone, it would help," I continued a little desperately.

James called from the bedroom. Stacy drank the rest of her tea and squeezed my hand. "You're sweet, Mom, but I think both Chris and I know we're a little past putting everything right over a nice weekend." Stacy jumped down from her stool and walked toward the kitchen door "After all," she said, "Chris is a very different type of dad."

I felt my blood drain, and then, all of a sudden, I was burning hot. I pulled open the robe I was wearing and fanned myself. Was this hot flashing or panicking? It was hard to know anymore. What would Stacy do when she found out he was on his way today?

I thought about calling Chris straight back and even picked up the receiver, but something inside me once again told me I was doing the right thing, and how could it be any worse than it was now? Instead, I called Martin. He picked up on the third ring. I looked at the clock. He'd probably just arrived at the office, since it was about a ten-minute trip for him.

"Hello, have I told you you've got to stop stalking me?" he said. "I know, you just can't live without me, and our home is just empty the minute I'm not there. I'm right, aren't I?"

"Yes, dear. You're so right. Martin, please tell me I'm doing the right thing."

"You're doing the right thing," he said. "Now, what is it you need me to reassure you about today? Staying married? Having the windows washed? Or changing the color of your hair?"

I smiled. I was always contemplating changing the color of my hair.

"You know," I said. "About Stacy and Chris."

"Oh," he said. "Meddling in other people's affairs." That kind of stung, but he followed it up with, "I think it's the kindest thing you could have done. I know how fond you are of Chris, and I feel that deep down, we both know that, for better or worse, they love each other, and all we have to do is show them that."

I nodded into the phone. "OK," I said, "you're right. Thanks, honey. You're the best."

"You're welcome. Now, if you're missing me anymore, there's a picture in the third drawer you took of me that morning we went camping—the one where I look like a homeless man. If you feel you need to call me again, put that up on the wall. That should change your mind and let me get a day's work done."

CHAPTER SIXTEEN

OOMPAH BANDS & SCARY REINDEER

After a few stops, Dan and the ladies of the Rejected Writers' Book Club arrived in Leavenworth at eleven a.m. and took in the full sight of the quaint, quirky town.

To attract tourists to this out of the way mountain resort, the community of Leavenworth had created a Bavarian wonderland right in the center of the Cascade Mountains. With snow on the peaks during the winter and a good chance of ground snow, it looked Christmassy and magical. The experience was enhanced by the Bavarian-style homes and shops, German food, and entertainment. It was utterly enchanting and gorgeous at Christmastime.

As the ladies and Dan pulled into the center of town, a German brass band could be heard blasting polka music from one of the twinkle-lit bandstands, and as they opened the car windows, the smell of sauerkraut and sausage greeted them.

"I do love it here," said Lavinia. "It's like going abroad without having to use your passport."

"It's surreal," said Dan. "I can see why Flora would like it here."

They rolled up to a hotel.

"I think we should get rooms," said Dan. "And then maybe we

can split up to find Flora. I don't know where the Nest is. When I looked online, I could only figure it was a nickname because I couldn't find it registered anywhere. We can ask in town and see if anyone knows about it."

"Sounds adorable," says Lavinia. "Can't wait to get into my snowsuit and start playing."

"We're looking for Flora," reminded Lottie, tapping her sister's arm. "We're not here to visit."

"I wonder if they'd let me ski naked?" asked Ruby thoughtfully.

"Oh my gosh," said Lottie. "That's the last thing anyone needs to see."

They walked into the hotel, and a strapping young man dressed in lederhosen greeted them at the check-in desk.

"Welcome to Leavenworth. How may I help you?"

"Well, I just might have to have you on a stick," said Lavinia. "Those shorts are adorable. You must be freezing in these temperatures."

He smiled as he reddened a little, unprepared for Lavinia's forthrightness. "I have to get used to it," he said. "Goes with the territory." He checked them all into their rooms and reminded them: "Tonight is the tree-lighting ceremony. It'll be beautiful, right in the middle of town."

"Hosted by the Von 'Tripp' singers, no doubt," said Lavinia sarcastically as they made their way to their rooms.

"Don't you mean Von Trapp?" Lottie inquired.

"Nope," said Lavinia. "After we've been here for a few hours with all that German beer sloshing about, I think I was right the first time!"

Once they were all in, they made their plans: they would separate to find Flora and meet back at the hotel later.

～

I SAT on tenterhooks waiting for Martin to arrive back from the airport at midday. I still hadn't told Stacy that Chris was on his way. I just couldn't quite find the right time. I was definitely having second thoughts. Stacy was curled up on the sofa, both twins newly bathed on her lap, and she was reading *If You Give a Mouse a Cookie* to them. Such a happy family picture.

I heard Martin's car arrive and went to meet them at the door. Martin walked in, said to me, "I'll be in my workshop if you want me," and disappeared. I could have killed him.

Chris stood sheepishly at the door.

"Hello, Mom," he said and gave me a hug. "How are you doing?" He looked pale and tired and sad. I followed Chris into the front room as he put down his bags, and the twins automatically jumped off the sofa to greet him.

"Daddy!" they shouted in unison.

Stacy's face was a picture. She went from shock to anger, and the first words out of her mouth were, *"What are you doing here?"*

Chris pulled both his children into his arms and hesitated to answer her.

"I invited Chris," I said, ready to take whatever was coming at me. "I think you two need to spend some time together, and your dad and I will take care of the twins while you do that."

Stacy picked up her cup of tea and stomped straight upstairs. Chris just shrugged his shoulders at me and settled himself down on the sofa to talk to the twins.

I tiptoed out to the workshop. Martin poked his head out the door. "Is it safe? Do I need to bring my tin helmet?"

"I've had an idea," I said.

"What? Another one? Is this as good as the last one?"

I smiled as I walked into his shed, shivering. "What if we were to take the twins away for an overnight like I was talking about the other day? Give Chris and Stacy a chance to figure this out? Dan thinks Flora might be up in Leavenworth and the Rejection Writers' Group told me they need my support. How about if we were to go up there and just hang out for the day? Take the kids sledding, and they can see the Christmas tree lighting. I think it'd be fun to take them to the snow."

"Do you remember who we're talking about?" said Martin. "We're talking about Poopy and Dribble. It's like trying to hammer jelly to a tree, keeping those two in line. Are you sure you want to throw snow and ice into the mix?"

"I know," I said. "But this is for Stacy."

Then to push him over the edge, I held up my casted arm.

Martin shook his head. "I'll go," he said reluctantly. "But I can't be sure of what you'll bring back."

"Great," I said. "I'll go and talk to Stacy about it."

I went back into the house. Chris had both children on his lap, and I could hear them chatting away to their dad. It was heartbreaking. I went upstairs and opened Stacy's bedroom door, expecting the onslaught of insults. Instead, she sat at the edge of her bed, crying.

"Oh, Stacy." I walked over to her and put my arms around her.

"Mom, I've made such a mess of my life. Everything seemed to be so simple just a few years ago, and now everything is upside down."

I hugged her tightly. "Children can do that to you. But listen. They are also going to give you the most joy you've ever had, as well as the most stress. It's hard when they're small and when you're so tired. But I think you really love Chris, and I think it's the stress of raising the children that's pushing you both apart. Please give your marriage a chance."

"How do you expect us to do that when the twins still need so much help and attention?" she snapped.

"Your dad and I have decided to take the twins on a little getaway. We're going to take them up to Leavenworth, where they can go sledding and play in the snow. They'll have a great time."

Stacy's face lit up. "You are? Are you sure Dad's OK with that?"

"He'll be fine," I said. "And members of the Rejected Writers' Book Club are up there to help play with the kids, so I don't want you to worry about us for a second. That will give you a chance to spend some time here on the island. You could go out for dinner, or you could just sit here and drink coffee, or sleep for two days, if that's what you really need. But at least you'll have some time to be together."

Stacy rubbed at her eyes. "You might be right, Mom. At least I should give it a shot. My heart ripped apart when I saw how excited the kids were to see him. After all, he is their daddy."

I smiled and nodded. "Why don't you go and spend some time with Chris and the kids?"

I went back into my bedroom, pulled out my suitcase, and, with my one arm, started to pack. Martin joined me.

"So," he said. "Are we all ready to go? Has World War III started down there or are we taking it with us to Leavenworth?"

I smiled. "Pack your skiwear," I said. "We're going."

"First, I don't have any skiwear," he said. "As you know, I can barely walk in a straight line. And second, recreation's the last thing I'm going to be doing. I'm going to be cutting up food for my wife in a cast and chasing two toddlers around while they try to eat snow."

"Hmm. Sounds about right," I said. "We'll set out straightaway."

~

MARTIN and I and Stacy's twins arrived in Leavenworth at about three o'clock. I called Lavinia.

"Hi, y'all," she said. "Why don't you come and join me in the oompah bar? They're singing carols in big poufy dresses. The good news is I'm also drinking schnapps, so it doesn't matter how bad they're singing is."

"I can't bring the twins into a tavern; maybe Martin can take the kids for a little while so I can meet with you," I said, looking over at him as we pulled into the hotel parking lot.

"Ooh, trains," shouted one of the twins. I looked out of the window. The Icicle Inn, which was where we were staying, had a mini train.

"Granddad would love to take you," I said as Granddad knotted his eyebrows at me. "Wouldn't you, Granddad?"

Martin huffed. "Looks like Granddad's going to spend a lot of time on the train," he noted as he watched the twins clap their hands in the back of the car.

We checked in as one twin pulled on each of our arms, saying in unison, "Train! Train! Train!"

"I'll pop off, meet with the ladies, and see if they've found Flora, then I'll call you in an hour and come and relieve you." I kissed Martin on the head. "By the way, I think you are wonderful." He gave me a reluctant smile back. As I disappeared from the hotel, I saw both twins pulling Martin toward the train, and I could hear him saying, "Wait a minute. Granddad's not as young as he used to be." He was going to have fun even though he was complaining—I could tell.

I met with the rest of the ladies, who had stopped to get something to eat in a little Bavarian bar, where an oompah band was in full swing. As I walked in, I practically collided with Lavinia.

"I could get into this," Lavinia shouted over the din, her arm locked with a person clad in Bavarian attire next to her as they swayed together to the music. "I feel like I'm in Germany."

I approached the table where the rest of the ladies sat. Annie was bobbing her head to the music as she knitted, and Lottie and Ruby were tucking into some German fare.

As I arrived at the table, so did Dan.

"Hi, Janet," he said, sounding tired. "Any luck?" he asked the group. He seemed oblivious to the upbeat Bavarian festivities going on all around him. They all shook their heads.

"Somebody said they think the Nest may be a place that's now called *the Nook*. The only way to get up there, though, is by sleigh. It's very steep and high in the mountains."

"How exciting," said Lottie. "I love a sleigh ride. I wish I'd thought to pack a muff."

My phone rang, and I stepped outside to answer it. It was Doris.

"How's it going? Did you find Flora yet?"

"We're still looking," I answered.

"I've got everything under control at home. Ethel, Momma, and I are on the road to join you for the evening to help find her. I have to be back first thing tomorrow, but we have the rest of the evening off."

"That'll be great," I said. "Then we'll have more chance of finding her."

About thirty minutes later, Doris arrived at the oompah bar.

"Any news?" she asked as she walked in.

"Not yet," I stated. "We have a lead on the place she might be staying at, so Dan is booking us a sleigh ride up there."

"Her phone is still off," said Dan. He sounded desperate. "What if she isn't even here in Leavenworth?" He shook his head, looking haggard.

"We're going to find her, Dan," I reassured him. "Please don't worry."

We arrived at the sleigh-ride port, where a someone dressed as a reindeer was waiting there to drive us. He put up his hands and shouted, "Frosty Knickers!"

That's a very odd way to greet us, I thought as we looked from one to the other. The reindeer ran toward us and threw his arms around the group in a big furry hug.

"They sure are friendly here in this little town," said Lavinia. "I've never been hugged by a reindeer before."

"It's me," said the muffled voice from inside the grinning reindeer costume. He pulled off his antlered head. We couldn't believe it—it was Ronald, the tramp we'd met back on the road trip two years before. We'd all been snowed in together at an old lodge.

Doris balked. "Well, I might have known you'd turn up like a bad penny."

"Ronald?" I asked. "What the heck are you doing in Leavenworth dressed as a reindeer?"

He giggled. "Ahh, got myself a job. Gave up the booze and decided to come clean. They let me be a reindeer here in this crazy town. Ain't it a kick? I'm the person taking you up on the sleigh," he said with a broad, gummy smile.

"Good grief," said Doris. "We're all going to die!"

"I sure missed you, Frosty Knickers," he said, tapping her face with his furry paw. "You, and these girls, and that apple pie. Where's the little skinny one?" he asked, looking around the group.

Dan looked down.

"We're hoping to find her," I said quickly. "We think she might be staying at the Nook."

"Well, I din't seen 'er, but I only just came on my shift. Come on, jump in," he said. "I'll give you the ride of your life."

"Why do I feel afraid?" said Doris as Ethel sucked air in through her teeth next to me.

Gracie said, "Ohh, I can't wait! It's like being Cinderella."

We jumped into the sleigh and wrapped ourselves under blankets on the seats.

Ronald shouted, "Hold onto your britches," and he took off like a rabid pack of wolves, with snow spraying in every direction.

"What was the last thing those horses pulled?" shrieked Doris. "A fire truck?"

He giggled, showing her another gummy smile. "I want to give you your money's worth," he shouted back over his shoulder before he encouraged the horses on faster.

"Where are the airbags?" asked Lavinia desperately.

"Or the seatbelts?" added Lottie.

"There's only one airbag," snipped Doris. "And he's driving the sleigh."

"I'm holding on for dear life," said Lavinia, grabbing hold of her twin. "I never thought my very last day would be spent on a sleigh in a fake Bavarian town, being pulled by a crazy reindeer that used to be a tramp."

We galloped up the side of the mountain until eventually we reached the door of a little blue-and-white wooden chalet-style building at the top.

We all got out, more than a little discombobulated.

"Here you are," Ronald said, jumping down. "Got ya' ere safe and sound, din't I?"

"I'm not sure we're either," said Doris, looking totally rattled. Ethel's hair was sticking straight up, and her face seemed to be locked in permanent shock. But Gracie just clapped her hands.

We got off our sleigh and made our way inside. The place was made completely out of logs, and it had possibly been a lodge in a former life. It was echoey and old. Large wool tapestries adorned the walls, as did an extensive collection of dusty German brass instruments. It smelled a little musty as we walked across the creaking floor toward the large oak welcome desk. I couldn't see any staff, just a map taped to the desk telling people which cabin was which.

"What do we do now?" asked Annie.

Suddenly, a man's face popped up from behind the counter. He had luminous eyes that were magnified by his Coke-bottle glasses. "Welcome to the Nook," he said, drawn out and solemnly.

I felt like I had walked into a funeral home. "How may I be of service?"

"I called earlier," said Dan. "I don't know if you remember me. I think there might be somebody staying here. My fiancée, Flora."

"*Flloorraa*," the clerk said, emphasizing her name. Then rolling each letter. "*Floor-raa. F-l-o-r-a.*"

We all stood there, looking at him. *Is he just going to say that over and over again like a parrot?* I wondered.

"Yes, we might have a *Flora*," he said, sounding unsure. "Let me look in the book. I can't read my writing, but I do know I have somebody in cabin four who is female."

"Well, that's a start," I said.

"Yes, yes, I have a couple in cabin five and a family of four in cabin two. So I guess Flora is the female in cabin three."

"You mean *four*," I stated.

"Yes," he said, nodding, agreeing with me. "Cabin four."

Doris rolled her eyes.

"Here's a map," he said, handing us a scribbling on a piece of paper.

"Who drew this for you?" Doris put on her reading glasses before turning it around in her hand. "That crazed reindeer out there?"

We all went outside and tried to find our way about, but the map was of no use. We wandered around for about twenty minutes, getting lost at every turn, until we finally located cabin four. The light was on, and a little red-and-white sign out front with the words "Welkom to zee Nook" written on it swung back and forth.

Dan hurried toward the door. Lavinia grabbed him by the arm before he made his way up the path.

"Maybe *we* should go and knock on the door first," she said. "Just in case . . ." Lavinia didn't finish the sentence, but we all knew what it meant.

He nodded, and Lavinia and Lottie made their way to the door.

Lavinia knocked on the door and smiled back at Dan, who hopped from foot to foot down at the bottom of the path. They waited, but no one came. She knocked again harder—still no reply.

"Looks like there's no one here," said Lottie despondently.

Dan looked crushed.

Ruby grabbed his arm. "Stay strong, man."

Lottie started to make her way back down the path but Lavinia stopped in her tracks. She moved back to the cabin.

Lottie shouted back to her, "Come on, Lavinia."

Lavinia ignored her.

"Lavinia!" repeated Lottie.

"*Shh,*" said Lavinia. "Listen."

They became quiet, and there it was: just the tiniest—but definite—sound of a cat meowing.

"I think it's Mr. Darcy," said Lavinia.

Dan couldn't wait any longer. He raced to the door and pressed his ear against it. As if on cue, Mr. Darcy jumped up on the window ledge, looked outside, and meowed.

Annie clapped. "It is Mr. Darcy! That means Flora is here somewhere."

"Yes, she is," said Dan, unable to contain the excitement in his voice. "Now all we have to do is find her."

We headed back to the chalet building, and the same man's head popped up again. He acted as if he hadn't met us before.

"Welcome, how may I be of service?"

"We were just here," said Doris gruffly. "Don't you remember us? We were looking for Flora."

"*Flloorraa,*" the clerk said again, exaggerating her name. "*F-l-o-r-a.*"

"Didn't we just do this routine?" stated Lavinia impatiently.

"Yes," he said. "She is in cabin four. Another group of people just went down to see her."

"That was us," said Lottie.

He blinked through his Coke-bottle glasses.

"She's not there," said Doris. "Do you know where she might be?"

He looked down at his book, saying the word *Flora* over and over again. "Oh yes, actually, I do know where she is—if she's the one with blonde hair. She booked a six thirty sleigh. She just left."

Dan looked exasperated.

"Can we book the next sleigh?" I asked before the group's foaming irritation erupted.

"Of course," he said. "It will be back in about thirty minutes. What name shall I book it under?"

"Janet," I responded.

"Jaaannettt," he said, overextending my name as he had Flora's.

Doris's eyes flicked to the ceiling. "Good grief."

"I like this guy," said Ruby. "He reminds me of the folks I hung out with in my serious pot-smoking days."

We all lined up in the reception chalet, sitting on hard wooden chairs and waiting for Ronald the Reindeer to return, with Bavarian polka music blaring overhead. It was cold and drafty, and the atmosphere was no warmer in the group. And Martin thought *he* had the hard end of the deal.

I called him while we waited and updated him. "How are the twins?" I asked.

"They've both passed out on the bed," he said. "And it only took fourteen trips on the train to do it."

"Are you OK?" I asked, concerned. "I can come back and relieve you if you need me to."

"No, you're fine," he said. "I'll call if I need rescuing. Right now, I'm having a whale of a time. I'm watching golf on TV, and I ordered myself room service—dinner and a scotch, which you can pay for when you get back."

I laughed. "I'll see you soon."

"Frosty Knickers!" said Ronald as he clapped eyes on Doris again. "Where are you and your bunch going now?"

"Back into town," said Doris sharply. "We need to find Flora."

Ronald roared with laughter and slapped his knee. "I thought that was her," he said. "She was all bundled up—just two eyes above a scarf. I only just dropped her off. What ja' guys playing, cops-n-robbers?"

"Did she mention where she was going?" asked Dan desperately.

Ronald took off his reindeer head and scratched at his greasy hair. "Something 'bout a coffee shop on the edge of town. Jump in an' I'll take you back," he said with his eyes glistening.

"Here we go again," said Lavinia as Ronald sped off with a loud *Yahoo!* "I didn't realize I would need my motion-sickness pills for Leavenworth."

When we arrived back in town, we didn't know what end of the main street she was at, so Dan, Doris, Ethel, and Gracie went one way while the twins, Ruby, Annie, and I went the other.

As we moved at a clip to the end of the road, we saw a sandwich board on the street in front of one of the coffee shops—written on it were the words *Poetry Reading Tonight*.

"Bingo," said Lavinia. "Lottie, Annie, and Ruby, you take one side of the room, and Janet and I will take the other."

As we walked around, I suddenly spotted a flow of pale blonde hair in the corner. It was her, curled up under one of her thick Victorian coats next to the fireplace, listening to someone reciting.

I couldn't believe we had found her. I stepped outside to call Dan.

CHAPTER SEVENTEEN

THE RUNAWAY BRIDE & ANOTHER CRAZY
SLEIGH RIDE

As Lavinia approached Flora, she noticed she was curled up like a baby, sleeping soundly. Probably exhausted by all the wedding preparations and the emotional upheaval. Lavinia knelt down beside her and stroked her hand gently.

"Flora, darling, are you awake?"

Flora's eyes fluttered open. She looked bewildered for a second, as if she were trying to remember where she was, and then the realization sent a cloud of sadness that passed across her face. She blinked her eyes, adjusting to the spotlight that was aimed at the stage but still in her direct view. Then she saw Lavinia leaning over her. That made her bolt upright.

"Are you Lavinia or Lottie?" she asked quickly.

"Lavinia, darling," she said. "And you shouldn't sit up quite so fast. You'll make yourself dizzy."

"What are you doing here?" she said sharply. "How did you find me?"

Lavinia sat down to join her at the table. "That's a long story, but more importantly, why are you here?"

Flora's face clouded over again, and she looked as if she was searching for the right words. Then she said in the tone of a young child, "I was kind of running away."

"Running away?" repeated Lavinia softly. "From what? Happiness? Don't you want to marry Dan?"

Flora winced at the sound of his name. "You don't understand," she said. "He won't want to marry me when he finds out the truth. I'm just saving him the bother of all that. I can look like the bad guy, and he can go back to Oregon and be OK."

"Well, you do have it all tied up in a neat little bundle," said Lavinia. "Unfortunately, people don't always do what we hope for in our own fantasies."

"You don't understand," said Flora. "I did something terrible; I didn't tell him the whole truth about my past. I didn't want him to think badly about me. When he finds out, he'll never forgive me."

Lavinia smiled. "Are you talking about your marriage to Andy?" she said quietly.

It was as if someone had thrown a bucket of ice water in Flora's face. She looked totally dumbstruck. "You know?" she whispered.

Lavinia nodded. "Yes, I know."

"So you understand why I had to leave Dan. Does he understand?" she added, eagerly.

"He doesn't know," answered Lavinia. "Lottie and I are the only ones who do. He's very concerned about you, Flora. He drove us up here to find you."

"Dan is here?" she asked with an eagerness she obviously—though poorly—tried hard to hide.

"Yes, he is," said Lavinia. "And there's something else you should know."

Lavinia never got any further in the conversation because someone else joined them at the table and whispered Flora's name.

Flora squinted up through the blaring spotlight.

"Dan?" she said breathlessly, like a child waiting for the much-anticipated return of a father. She got to her feet as the person walked forward. The spotlight aimed toward the stage continued to silhouette him in front of them. Flora furrowed her brow. Lavinia squinted, too. Yes, this was a man, but he looked shorter than Dan. Much more squat. It couldn't be, could it? But it wasn't until he spoke again that they both knew who it was.

"Flora, I'm sorry. I am so sorry I did this to you."

Flora turned to him. "It was you! You sent me that letter! You were the person who wanted me to send you money."

John stepped forward as Lavinia's eyes acclimated to the light. She noticed he, too, had aged ten years over the past week.

"Yes, Flora, and I felt terrible about it. You have no idea."

Flora was boiling, and Lavinia could sense she was about to spill over.

"Now, Flora, wait a second. Hear him out. There's more to this story."

Suddenly, there was another set of footsteps behind them. And then the unmistakable voice of Lavinia's twin:

"Lavinia, did you find her? I've recited all my prayers, and I still haven't seen her." Lottie stepped toward the table and nearly collided with John, who was still standing in front of Flora. She, too, was blinded by the spotlight and saw only a silhouette. "Lavinia Marie Labette, don't tell me you're sitting here with a man! Heaven preserve us, I leave you for two minutes, and already you're in trouble."

"My darling," said Lavinia. "I have three of them here with me."

Lottie's outburst and Lavinia's response could do nothing but lighten the mood. Lottie used her hand to shade her eyes and said, "Well, this isn't a man at all. It's John!"

"Thanks," said John dryly.

"You know what I mean," said Lottie. "What in heaven's name are you doing up here?"

"I found Flora," said Lavinia, eying their young friend, who now sat looking crushed.

"Praise be to God!" said Lottie, squinting and shielding her eyes again. "Where is she?"

"Right here next to me."

They all took their time to hug Flora and surrounded her at the table.

"But, John, what are you doing here? I thought you were long gone. How did you know we were coming here or that Flora was here?"

"I saw Lavinia on the ferry," explained John. "She tried to convince me to come with her, to tell Flora what happened."

"So," said Lottie, crossing her arms, "that is whom you were with on the ferry. I knew that a man must have fit into your plan somehow."

"I'm not a man," said John. "Remember?"

"But why did you run away?" asked Lottie as she sat next to Flora. "You're due to get married the day after tomorrow. We could have at least tried to sort out this mess at home."

"You all have to know there was nothing between Andy and me, and we were just really good friends. He needed help, but I never told Dan . . ." Her voice trailed away.

"Never told Dan! What?" said a voice from behind them. Everyone jumped. They hadn't heard the person approach the table, but he was plainly silhouetted in front of them now, and by the outline, it was clearly Dan.

Flora jumped to her feet and threw her arms around his neck and held him tight. He held her for a second, then pulled her out of the embrace.

"Didn't tell me what?" he asked again. Lavinia could tell by his tone he was hurt.

"That I've been married," she said quietly. "And now it looks like I might still be married."

Dan jumped back as though someone had slapped his face. He shook his head in disbelief.

"What did you . . . Married? What do you . . ." He couldn't seem to get a whole sentence out to make something cohesive. Finally, he said, "Flora? You . . . you . . . are married?"

Flora nodded. He took another step back from her. This wasn't going to go well, and Lavinia had had enough of this type of conversation in her own life to see that this young man was on the brink.

"It's not the way it sounds, Dan," said Lavinia, reaching the young couple's side. "Don't go jumping to the wrong conclusions. Flora did something in her youth, something that was just a little naive, but haven't we all done that at some time? I'm sure you did stupid things when you were young." She babbled on as his face grew red with anger.

"I once knocked a nest of birds out of a tree," he said coldly. "But I didn't get married." He was now pacing, each step landing harder against the hardwood floor. "I came here afraid you'd gotten cold feet and that somehow it was my fault. I thought you didn't want to get married or you didn't love me. Now I find out that you've been—that you might still be—married? I can't believe you, Flora."

John jumped to his feet and walked toward the three of them. "Please don't blame Flora. It's all my fault."

Dan, who hadn't noticed John, suddenly put two and two together and made ten.

"You and Flora?" His eyes blazed. "You and Flora are married?" Dan stepped toward John and raised his arm. Everyone, including John, was sure he was going to punch him, but instead, Dan balled up both fists and spat out, "I hope you'll both be very happy together." And then he turned on his heels and exited the coffee shop.

Flora went to run after him, but Lavinia stopped her. "Let him be." She took Flora by both shoulders. "He's upset and needs to let off some steam. He'll be more rational once he's done that. In the meantime, we need to get you back home. There are an awful lot of people arriving in Southlea Bay for a wedding the day after tomorrow, and no matter what happens, someone has to figure this thing out. Let's get you packed so we can get back first thing tomorrow morning."

"But what about Dan?" Flora's heart sounded like it was breaking.

Lottie came around the other side of her, supporting her since she looked as if she would pass out at any minute. "Come on, honey, let's get you back to your place," she said. "I've been through more than one heartache with Lavinia. I know exactly what you need, and first thing is a strong cup of tea."

"But I have to talk to Dan. I have to explain everything," she continued desperately.

"Let me talk to him once he's calmed down," said Lavinia.

They all helped Flora to the door.

Suddenly, Doris, Ethel, and Gracie, appeared in the doorway. Doris was puffing and blowing, her face bright red. "There you all are. Dan got a phone call and dashed off before he could even tell us where he was going. Any luck?"

"We found Flora," said Lottie despondently.

"Wonderful," said Doris. "So where's Dan?"

"He's gone," said Ruby.

"Gone, what do you mean *gone*? What's wrong with young people these days? Don't they want to be together?"

Flora burst into tears.

We all got back on the sleigh and Ronald shook his head at all the solemn faces. "Did somebody die?" He sucked on his gums.

"Not yet, but Rudolph just might unless you drive this sleigh with more caution," warned Doris sternly.

"Nonsense," he said, slipping on his reindeer head. "What you people need is some livening up."

He pulled the reins and off we went again, dashing through the snow.

"Good grief," said Lottie. "I don't think any of my bones will ever be in the same place again."

We huddled together as Flora sobbed quietly in the middle of our group.

~

BACK AT THE NOOK, they were a very somber bunch as Flora pulled all her clothes together and placed them in her ancient carpetbag.

About an hour later, they heard a shout from Ruby, who sat under a sheepskin blanket out on the deck. "He's back!"

They all peered out the window and noticed a figure striding through the snow toward the cabin.

Flora's hands fluttered to her chest, and Lottie shouted, "Hallelujah!"

Dan arrived at the cabin and sat down outside on one of the chairs on the deck without saying anything.

"I'll go get logs for the fire," said Ruby, who didn't appear to know much about dealing with heartbroken young men. However, Lavinia knew all about the subject, and so she walked out onto the deck to sit next to him. He looked devastated.

"Hey, Dan," she said. "How are you doing?"

"How do you think I'm doing?" he snapped back. He sounded bitter. "I just found out the girl I'm going to marry is already married."

Lavinia tapped his hand. "Now, that's not exactly true. Don't be so hard on her. There is more to this story."

Flora crept out onto the deck as well. Dan stood up stiffly, and it looked as if he just wanted to get away.

"Dan," Flora said softly. "Please don't leave. We need to talk about this."

"Congratulations on your marriage." The sarcasm and hurtful delivery just didn't sound right coming out of Dan's mouth. "I just came up here to find out why you lied to me."

She appeared to find her deepest courage and placed her hand on his arm. He looked as if he couldn't bear it any longer. He took her in his arms and held her like it was going to be the last time. Tears shone clearly in both of their eyes.

Lavinia excused herself and made her way back into the house. As she opened the bedroom door, she nearly tripped over her sister, who was on her knees in fervent prayer.

"Good idea," said Lavinia. "I might join you."

"I'm not sure God will know who you are," answered Lottie, a smile creeping onto her face.

"I'll tell him I'm you," said Lavinia. "He'll never know the difference. That's how I'm planning on getting into heaven, by the way."

Lottie opened one eye and gave her sister such a scowl that Lavinia had to laugh.

"How are we doing out there?" asked Lottie.

"Not good," said Lavinia. "I'm not sure they're going to make it. Dan is very hurt."

Lottie nodded sadly and went back to praying.

CHAPTER EIGHTEEN

YODELING HEATHENS & SKELETONS OUT THE CLOSET

Dan let go of Flora and walked to the edge of the deck. He was openly crying now, and his heart felt like it was breaking as he looked absently out toward the mountains. It had just started to snow again.

Flora joined him at his side. "You've got to understand, I never meant to hurt you. That marriage was all a mistake."

Dan winced deep inside every time she said the word *marriage*. He was reminded it had taken place. He kept hoping that maybe there'd been a mistake. That somehow, this had been a mix-up. But hearing her talk about it now made it feel real and harsh to him.

Flora continued, "Dan, you have to believe me. This was a long time ago, when I was still in college."

"No one marries someone by mistake, Flora," he responded coldly, cutting her off.

"But it was! Sit down, Dan. I'm going to tell you everything. Then, if you want to, you can leave me."

Dan hesitated for a moment before he sat down. Flora sat next to him and tried to take his hand. He pulled it away and sat back in his chair.

She sighed and started her story. "I met Andy when I was getting my art degree. Do you remember? I told you, I spent a year there, in Canada."

He nodded. "Painting murals, I remember. What I don't remember is the part where you added, 'By the way, I also got married.'"

Flora looked at him in exasperation. "Dan, you're not making this any easier for me." He folded his arms, and she started again. "I met Andy the first week at the university, and he needed a teacher's assistant at home for his business. I was a foreign student with a lot of free time, so I volunteered and started working for him, and we became really good friends. He was very kind to me."

"'And the next thing you know we were in love,'" said Dan, sarcastically finishing her sentence.

"No," said Flora, getting annoyed. "It wasn't that kind of relationship. He was very respectful of me and loved my work, and I liked him and helped him with his. While we were working together, he got an incredible job offer in the United States. I mean, the job of a lifetime. But then he heard from the company that they had tried to apply for a visa for him, and it had failed. So they were going to have to offer it to someone else. He was heartbroken. I took him out for dinner to try to cheer him up, but there was no consoling him. In the end, we went back to his house."

"I know where this is going, and I'm not interested in hearing the details of your love affair."

"No, you don't. You don't know anything. Dan, please listen. We went back to his house, and he opened a bottle of wine, and you know I hardly drink. We talked late into the night, and about two in the morning, we came up with this crazy idea. What if I was to marry him for a green card? He could apply and still get his job. Well, in the middle of the night and in the throes of my youth, it didn't seem like a big deal. It would just be a marriage on paper, after all. Then after he got the job and everything was finalized, we'd just file for a quiet annulment.

"So that's what we did. We had a quick wedding a few days later and asked a couple of people off the street to be our witnesses, and that was supposed to be that.

"He did get his job and was so excited, and we filed for the annulment. But before I got the paperwork, well . . . that's when Dad got sick and I had to rush home. After that, my life was a blur. When it did cross my mind, there were always weightier things to deal with: doctors, hospitals, funerals . . ." Her voice trailed off.

"Anyway, I realized as our wedding got closer that I wasn't sure that it had been resolved. So a few months ago, I contacted his old address in Canada, and there was someone there who knew of him but didn't know where he was. They said they'd heard he was getting married soon to some girl in Georgia, where he had taken his job. That put my mind at rest because if he was still married to me, then he couldn't do that and I thought that settled it.

"Until the other day. That's when I got the letter through the post that said I was still legally married to Andy, and there was a copy of the marriage certificate inside it. I panicked. It was the first time I'd ever seen it up close, and looking at it—it looked so official, it made me realize that I might be in a lot of trouble if I married you. So I ran away. I know that was ridiculous, but honestly, I was just hoping you wouldn't hate me or something and that we wouldn't have to do this."

"But why didn't you tell me?" Dan ran his hands through his hair. "Do you have any idea how much it's hurt me that you didn't trust me to tell me all this? How many other things have you hidden from me?"

Flora flushed. "I promise this is the one and only skeleton in my closet, and up until the other day, I thought it wasn't even one of those."

"Marriage is something big, Flora, and the fact that you treated this so lightly makes me wonder how committed you are to our relationship."

Dan's words hit Flora full force, and she sank into her chair.

He got up and started to pace. "But how did all this come to light?" he said. "Who sent you the letter?"

"It was John," she murmured.

"Why would he do that?"

"Money," she responded quietly.

Dan shook his head. "I need to get away and think. I'm not sure what all this means for me, much less what it means for us. I don't know if I can get past the fact that you lied to me."

Alarmed, Flora raced up to him and grabbed desperately at his arm. "But you still love me, right?"

Dan pulled away from her. "I don't know, Flora. I just don't know anything anymore."

He needed to breathe, needed to walk. He got up and walked away from the cabin. He heard Flora's steps running up behind him, and then Lavinia's voice: "Let him go, honey."

Flora's voice drifted out toward him as he walked away into the cold stillness: "Did you hear what he said? He said he didn't love me."

That was the last thing Dan heard as he headed toward the sleigh.

~

DAN ENTERED the Edelweiss Bar and ordered a couple of drinks. The town was packed, alive with people all there to celebrate the lighting of the tree, which was now illuminated with hundreds of colored bulbs. Below it, people huddled around a chestnut roast and sang Christmas carols. He had just ordered his third whiskey when Lavinia joined him at the bar.

"Hey there," she said, pulling herself up on the stool next to him. Then she waved to a rather buxom barmaid wearing traditional Bavarian clothes. "I will have whatever he's drinking." The barmaid put a whiskey right in front of her, and Lavinia toasted Dan, saying, "Bottoms up!" She threw it back in one slug.

Dan watched her, impressed.

"You know," she said, "I was always able to drink my second husband under the table, but I'm hoping you won't put me to the test on that. I'm not as good with getting over hangovers as I used to be." She ordered them both another one and knocked hers back. "Now, we need to figure out what we're going to do."

"I know what I'm going to do," responded Dan, coldly. "I'm going to go home, tell everyone the wedding's off because, unfortunately, my bride is inconveniently already married."

"Why, yes, you could do that, but what would that achieve? You would embarrass her, but at the end of the day, all that matters is whether you love each other, and I know you do." Lavinia ordered another whiskey. Dan did, too, and they both knocked them back. "You do love her, don't you, Dan?"

Dan's face softened before he answered, "I do, but what does it matter? She's already married."

"That's where you are in luck," said Lavinia. "You were in such a flap, you didn't stop to listen to John. She isn't still married; he was just going to blackmail her into thinking she was. You know how gullible she is. He was just trying to make a buck. But I have the final paperwork right here." She pulled out the manila envelope and handed it to Dan before they both slugged back another slug. "What you've got to decide is whether you can forgive her."

"I don't know what to do," he said desperately. "Of course I love her, but I can't believe she lied to me about this. I'm just not sure she is the person I fell in love with."

Lavinia took his hand. "I've known Flora for a long time, and believe me, she has no crazy side life, and you couldn't meet a sweeter, kinder, lovelier person. I think you would regret walking away from her, Dan. Not tomorrow or the next day, while your pride is so hurt—but in time, you would."

~

THAT EVENING, I crept into our hotel room to check on the babies and Martin and found them all sleeping soundly. Not an hour later, I was getting ready for bed when I got a call from Doris, and I made my way to the foyer, where she'd arranged an emergency meeting.

She sucked in her cheeks and blew out air, sitting there staunchly, wearing her nightgown, her hair already wrapped in curlers. Ethel sat pursed faced beside her.

"If we don't do something, this whole wedding could be off," Doris said.

"I do hope not," said Gracie, who had changed into her Tinkerbell onesie and sat curled up in a chair next to a roaring wood fire.

Ruby nodded. "That boy is having second thoughts for sure." She wore a lemon-colored robe, and I was pretty sure she was naked underneath.

"Lottie is staying with Flora this evening to keep her comfortable, and Lavinia has disappeared," Doris said. "Big surprise there—no doubt dancing and singing around the Christmas tree with a bunch of men, wearing those little tight shorts." She *hmphed*. "I had planned an early night, but I just checked on Dan's room again and he's still not back, so we might need to get ourselves dressed and go back out there to find him."

I sighed, beginning to feel like a private detective. This felt like some sort of manic farce: first looking for the bride, now the bridegroom.

"I know we all thought we were off to bed," Doris continued decisively. "But we need to get dressed and save this wedding!"

Twenty minutes later we had dressed and split up and were

making our way through the throngs of people as we looked for Dan.

I entered a tiny bar that was painted Bavarian style and was automatically hooked into a drinking circle. People swayed, holding big tankards of beer in their hand. Some sort of musical entertainment kept the patrons preoccupied at the front of the bar, although *musical* was a loose term. It sounded like someone had stepped on a cat's tail.

As I desandwiched myself from a rather rotund blond man wearing a little green felt hat with a feather stuck in it, I caught sight of Lavinia, up on the stage with a mic in her hand. She was the wailing cat. I moved closer to the stage to see exactly what she was doing when I saw a sign that read "Yodeling Competition." As the crowd applauded Lavinia's ear-bleeding performance, she handed the mic to Dan, who then started his own bloodcurdling rendition of the yodel. In between scaring small children, the two of them laughed hysterically. Both of them were blind drunk!

Suddenly, the rest of the ladies were behind me, Doris dressed but still in her curlers.

"Well, I never," she said with a huff.

Beside her, I thought Ethel was going to have a kitten. "Heathens," she said under her breath.

Doris barreled toward the stage and promptly removed Lavinia from it.

"Sorry, I have to go," said Lavinia into the mic as she was pulled away. "My mom is here to take me home." She descended into raucous laughter.

We carried a drunk Dan and Lavinia back to the hotel, the two of them straddled between all of us. When we got Dan to his room and threw him onto his bed, Lavinia automatically started to curl up next to him.

"Oh no you don't," I said, picking her back up. "This relationship is complicated enough as it is without there being speculation about another woman." I practically had to carry Lavinia on my back to her room, where I deposited her on her own bed.

Exhausted, I arrived back at my room just before midnight. Martin stirred as I walked in.

"Did you have a fun evening?" he said and yawned.

"Oh, it was a barrel of laughs, believe me. I would rather have been going around on that train all night."

CHAPTER NINETEEN

A RUNAWAY BRIDEGROOM &
GINGERBREAD BONDING

Lottie and Flora had caught the morning sleigh down to join us for breakfast. Mr. Darcy mewed and cried from his cat carrier beside them.

"Flora is coming back to Southlea Bay with us," Lottie stated. "She needs to get ready for her wedding tomorrow."

Everyone shifted uneasily.

Flora scanned all the faces eating breakfast, but Dan hadn't joined us yet.

When Lavinia arrived, she was wearing dark sunglasses and ambling very slowly.

"Oh, what I wouldn't do to have the constitution of someone twenty years younger. You know—someone fifteen," she said in an attempt at a joke, but then laughing at her joke caused her to wince in pain and hold her head.

Lottie sighed. "I can't believe you went drinking, Lavinia Marie. Especially with that young man."

After making more than their fair share of a maple-syrup mess, our grandbabies wanted one last go on the train, and Gracie was more than happy to go with them. I saw her tiptoeing away with Annie as they went off for their ride.

Doris marched off to rouse Dan, but five minutes later, she bustled back, her face etched with concern.

"He's gone already," she said. "Apparently, he checked out two hours ago and took the train back to the island ferry."

Flora looked distraught. I grabbed her hand. "Don't worry, he just needs some space. We'll see him when we get back home.

~

JUST AFTER MIDDAY, Martin and I arrived back with the twins and entered the totally, eerily silent cottage.

"Mommy, we're home," sang Livvy. Her brother, whose vocal skills weren't quite as developed as his sister's, echoed something similar.

I crept up the stairs and tiptoed into Stacy's room to find both her and Chris, asleep in each other's arms. I felt my heart stir. This had to be a good sign.

Moving back downstairs, I kept the twins occupied by making a gingerbread house until their parents woke two hours later.

The twins ran to greet them and pulled them toward the table.

"House, Momma, house," said Livvy as James bounced up and down.

Stacy hugged them both.

"Let's see what you have been making with Grandma," she said, giving me a heartfelt hug. She whispered in my ear, "Thanks, Mom, for everything."

I felt my eyes tear up.

Chris arrived down the stairs, lifted James, and went over to look at the house. They interacted with their children in that easygoing way that assured me things were better between them.

Later, once the twins and Chris had gone out to see Grandpa's model trains in his workshop, Stacy curled up on the sofa with a cup of tea.

I didn't even have to broach the subject. She brought it up.

"It's amazing what a night of eight hours' sleep will do," she said with a yawn. "I can't believe how wonderful being awake feels."

I joined her on the sofa. "You and Chris both look a lot better."

She grabbed my hand. "We talked for hours, more than we've talked in the last eighteen months. I realized so much of the resentment I was feeling toward him was actually toward motherhood. I love the kids with my whole heart, you have to know that. But I need more."

"Of course," I said, nodding as I took a sip of my tea.

"And so, I've decided to go back to work. Just part time, but as soon as we made the decision, I felt this whole weight lift from my shoulders. I always thought I would have a nanny, but when we nearly lost them early in the pregnancy and then with them being preemies, I just didn't feel I could trust anyone else with them."

"The Momma Bear instinct." I smiled. "I remember it well."

"Working again is right for me, and it's right for our family," she said. "I know I will be a much better mother and wife if I'm not always so worn out."

I stroked her hand. "You look so much better. What about you and Chris?"

"Chris is going to talk to his boss about not traveling so much, and my extra income should take a lot of pressure off him doing overtime. And we are going to start having date nights.

"We went out for dinner in town last night, and I couldn't believe how wonderful it was to laugh with him again, not to mention eating a whole meal while it was still hot. We were like newlyweds." Her eyes welled with tears. "It's been so hard, Mom; I didn't realize until the twins weren't here."

I put down my tea and hugged her. As she sobbed into my

shoulder, she said, "I had no idea what an amazing mom you were until I tried to do this job. And now I know. I know I really didn't appreciate you until I had the kids. I love you and Dad so much."

I hugged her tightly and started to cry, too. She had no idea how long I had wanted to hear those words.

As the men arrived back in with the twins, they found us there, sobbing. Martin stopped dead. "Who died while we were gone? We only left you for twenty minutes."

I blew my nose and dismissed him with a wave of my hand. "No one, we're just bonding, that's all."

He shook his head. "Isn't that what me and Chris were doing in the workshop? I didn't feel the need to soak his shirt in the process."

CHAPTER TWENTY

A SCARY SINGER & A BEAR WITH RINGS

In the morning, the ladies of the Rejected Writers' Book Club arrived at Flora's cottage, whispering in hushed tones in the kitchen.

"I've tried to put off people's questions about Flora and Dan," I informed them. "I have just been telling people they were having some time apart from each other before the wedding."

"Do you think they'll go through with it?" whispered Annie.

"I'm not sure at this point," I said. "We'll just keep moving ahead and hope for the best."

By midmorning, dressed in her bridal gown, Flora was the saddest bride that we'd ever seen. We all tried to cheer her spirits.

Lottie hugged her. "Come on, Flora. It's going to turn out OK. Dan is a smart man. He'll come around."

When Martin and our twin grandbabies arrived, Livvy and James tore around the house in their wedding clothes. Ten minutes before she was to leave for the wedding, Flora walked out onto the sidewalk. From all around, groups of neighbors had gathered together to get a glimpse and a photo of the bride as she left. Flora was nervous, but she also seemed touched by their presence. It was as if she'd forgotten that to all these people, she

195

was part of their family. She climbed in the car, and Martin slid in beside her. He seemed in his usual jovial mood and cracked jokes as we sat waiting for the chauffeur. He was to arrive with Flora.

As I made my way toward my car with our twins, Doris arrived with Ethel and Gracie by her side. She grabbed my arm and hissed, "The groom isn't there. I suggest you get that chauffeur to drive very slowly to the Labettes'."

I nodded and had a quiet word with the driver. The car pulled away at a snail's pace as neighbors cheered and threw confetti.

I arrived ahead of them, and even though the chauffeur drove slowly, when they arrived at the Labettes' garden fifteen minutes later, there was still no sign of Dan. The wedding guests seemed relieved to see the bride arrive at least, but the whole topic of conversation circling the grounds and in the chapel, was about the groom, or the lack of him.

We got out of the cars, and Flora was ushered into the gardens for some pre-wedding photos, and then went to the downstairs parlor, where she'd be waiting until the start of the wedding. Flora walked into the hallway and grabbed Lavinia's arm. "Is he here?"

Lavinia shook her head. "I'm sorry, honey, he hasn't arrived yet. But we've sent Ruby over there. You just sit tight for a while."

I walked into the little white chapel, and it was magical. At the front, a newly cut spruce tree took up the whole corner, its fresh piney scent mingling with the jasmine from the candles that decorated the aisle and creating an intoxicating aroma. It stood about twelve feet to the ceiling and was decorated with satin ribbons and baubles in Flora's pink and mauve colors. Hanging throughout the branches, crystal icicles glimmered against tiny white lights and miniature bride and groom ornaments hung on long silver strands. Flowers of Flora's choice had been threaded into long garlands and completed the decorations of the tree. About the room, winter plants and white and pink poinsettias were everywhere. At the far end, in the arched window with its stunning vista of the rolling blue waves of the Sound, was a huge bouquet of fragrant white lilies.

As I tiptoed down the aisle with the twins to find Stacy, I looked at all the eager and expectant faces. Everyone I knew and loved was there.

Ernie smiled at me and patted my hand as I passed him. He sat near the back, wearing a dapper brown suit with a white flower in his buttonhole. Next to him was Mrs. Bickerstaff, her face pinched in concern. The next row down, Annie sat next to Ethel and Gracie. Gracie wore a pink fairy costume and her signature boa, and Ethel, a no-nonsense suit. Behind them, on the end of the aisle, was our hypochondriac costumer from the show the year before, June Horton. She had her usual plastic shopping bag tucked between her legs on the floor and was sucking on one of her cough sweets.

"I won't shake hands with you," she whispered to me as she grabbed my arm. "I think I've got the flu." I nodded uneasily as I held my breath through a clenched smile.

Stacy, behind June, reached out for me, and I handed her the twins. She was lovely in a periwinkle-blue dress, and Chris looked handsome by her side in a gray suit. I told her it might be a little late starting, so I would come back for the twins. She nodded, and she and Chris took a twin each and put them on their laps.

As I moved back up the aisle, I waved to Karen, my library manager. Dan's parents sat on the other side, looking very elegant next to a very overdressed and bored-looking Marcy. Dan's mom gave me a strained smile.

I made my way back to the house to wait with the wedding party and noticed Doris parading up and down in front of the main gates in her robes.

Fifteen minutes later, we were still waiting.

"We need to do something about the guests." Lottie rubbed

her hands together nervously. "They're starting to get antsy in there."

"I know: I'll sing them a song," said Lavinia decisively. Everyone in the room stopped for a minute and stared at her.

Lottie was the first to speak. "Lavinia, honey, you might not remember this, but you don't sing."

"So now would be a good time for me to learn," she answered, making her way out to the garden. "Don't you think?"

I followed her cautiously. As I reentered the chapel, Gladys arrived behind me. She was dressed in a mishmash ensemble that looked as if she'd thrown it together at the last minute, and I wasn't sure she had even been invited. She nudged me as I hovered about at the back of the room and asked me in a very loud voice, "Did the groom ditch her? I have big money riding on this. I've come to collect my—" She stopped short when she caught sight of Lavinia, who had now found a microphone.

"Hi, y'all. I'd like to thank you for coming. There's been a little bit of a delay, so I've decided to sing you a little song until we can get things moving."

"Good grief," said Gladys. "Doesn't she know everyone is already in enough pain?" Wide-eyed, she slipped into the back pew to watch the car wreck.

Olivia, the music director from our show the year before, was seated two rows down from the back, dressed in a lovely high-waisted red lace dress, with one of her pearl-and-velvet chokers. She turned to me, alarm registering on her face. She had tried to have Lavinia sing a solo in our show and had given up, declaring her tone deaf. And now she was going to sing. Yodeling aside, no one had ever heard Lavinia sing a song in public before, but once she started, no one was ever going to want to hear Lavinia sing again.

Lavinia said something to the pianist, who eyed her distrustfully but reluctantly started to play. Then Lavinia took up her mic and started singing: *"See the pyramids along the Nile, watch a sunrise on a tropical isle . . ."*

Having more than my fill of the painful performance, I crept back to the house to check on Flora. I opened the door just as Lavinia belted out the chorus: *"Just remember, you belong to me."*

"Oh dear God," said Lottie, going pale. "She thinks she's Patsy Cline."

It was as Lavinia was hitting the high notes in the second verse that Flora stood up and made a decision. "This has gone far enough," she said. "I'm going to go in there. If Dan is not coming, then I'm going to tell everyone."

As she threw back her veil, Lottie called out to heaven, "Oh God, we need your strength."

Flora reached the chapel just as Lavinia belted out the last line, which was met with a mixture of shock and gratefulness that it was all over as the congregation clapped despondently.

The doors flew open, and Flora marched down the aisle with determination.

$\sim$

Mrs. Hemlock, who had been commissioned by Doris to play for the wedding, had been watching the proceedings with interest. It was indeed an unusual wedding. For one thing, neither the bridegroom nor the best man were waiting at the front, and now this odd woman and her performance were starting the ceremony.

She suddenly noticed the bride moving toward her.

Mrs. Hemlock started to play the Wedding March but noticed that Flora seemed to be taking the march literally. She'd never seen a bride come down the aisle at such a clip. She obviously really wanted to get married.

But to whom? thought the pianist as her fingers flew over the keys, trying to keep up with the bride's brisk pace. Mrs. Hemlock shook her head. She hoped it wasn't going to be odd, like one of those modern weddings where people got dressed up as Star Trek characters and the grooms sang like Elvis. It was all very unsettling, and here today, a bride was galloping down the aisle without even a groom to come to. She continued to speed up, playing as fast as she could to match Flora's long strides. She'd only just gotten to her third bar before Flora was at the front. *No,* she thought as she sighed, *these modern weddings stink.*

Flora turned to face the crowd. They all looked up at her in smiling anticipation. The brides voice shook as she tried to speak.

"Hello," she said. "I'm sorry you've all been sitting here, but there is something I need to tell you."

Suddenly, the chapel door flung open and ricocheted off the back wall, and Doris came galloping down the aisle, her white robes flapping up and down like a distressed seagull.

Mrs. Hemlock started to play the music again. She had played for a lot of gay weddings lately and she didn't like to judge anyone, but these two sure were an odd couple. She started to play from where she'd left off. She once again had to hurry her pace, as Doris was also moving at a clip, followed by another young man.

Oh, thought Mrs. Hemlock, *maybe this is the groom or the best man?* He seemed to be running to catch up with Doris. Then another woman ran in, grabbed two children, and hustled them back out again. Why were all these people rushing around so much? It wasn't like marriage was going to go out of fashion.

The woman in the robes got to the front, grabbed the bride by the arm, and whispered something into her ear.

The bride flushed. She pulled back down her veil and stepped back up the aisle at a more orderly pace, smiling nervously to people as she made her way.

This threw Mrs. Hemlock for a loop. Should she play the exit music or the entrance music? These people were coming and going like no tomorrow, and as far as she could fathom, a wedding hadn't even taken place.

Suddenly, another tall man with dark curly hair and emerald eyes raced in and up the aisle. Mrs. Hemlock threw her hands up in despair. This young man stopped and met the bride halfway.

The whole room heard the bride say through newly glistening tears, "You came."

"I did."

Mrs. Hemlock sat with her hands hovering over the keys. She really wasn't sure what to play. She thought for a minute of playing a reprise of "You Belong to Me" but was afraid that frightful woman would get up and sing again. Besides, she wasn't sure who belonged to whom.

"See you in a minute," said the bride, grabbing and squeezing his arm.

"Yes," he said, turning to her.

"I love you," she shouted behind her as she exited the chapel. It was loud enough that everyone heard it and clapped while the groom joined the best man at the front of the aisle.

Mrs. Hemlock shook her head and pulled out a magazine. She wasn't going to play another note until somebody told her what she was supposed to be playing. She wasn't a mind-reader, for goodness sake.

As the groom straightened up at the front of the aisle, money passed hands in the congregation behind him as bets were collected. The groom had indeed shown up. The optimists had won.

~

WE ALL MOVED into the garden and watched from the doorway as Doris made her way into the chapel . . . again. She was out of breath and red in the face, but she did her best to look solemn as she placed her hands together and walked prayerfully down the aisle.

Doris nudged Mrs. Hemlock, and "The Wedding March" started for the third time. Livvy tripped down the center of the aisle as we had practiced with her at home, throwing handfuls of petals and keeping a few to put into her mouth as she went. Everybody gushed at how cute she was. *One down, one to go,* I thought.

I gave James his pink velvet cushion to hold with the two rings firmly tied to it. "Remember," I instructed him, "you are the ring bearer. It's a very important job. You have to give this cushion to the man right at the front." James's eyes grew wide, and even as small as he was, he seemed to understand the gravity of his job.

Coyly, he started toddling down the aisle, and then suddenly, he turned to the people on the left and started growling and fixed his little hand into a clawlike shape. Then he continued down the aisle and did the same to the people on the right.

"What is he doing?" Martin asked as we watched him.

"I have no idea." I shook my head.

He made it as far as his mother, who leaned out to him, I assumed to ask him the same question. "I'm the ring bear!" he shouted out.

The whole congregation sniggered as he continued down the aisle, growling all the way to the front.

Lavinia and Lottie headed down the aisle, looking as impeccable as always. Then, lastly, Martin and Flora.

"Are you ready?" Martin asked quietly.

She nodded, her eyes still glowing with tears.

As they made their way down the aisle, I slipped into the pew at the back of the church next to Ernie, who tapped my hand and beamed. "Don't they make a lovely couple?" he whispered as Flora moved to Dan's side.

"They sure do," I answered him.

As they stood at the front of the tiny chapel, Doris conducted the wedding and, with all the upheaval, stuck adamantly to Flora's agreed service—dead poets and all. It was obvious to me she didn't want to rock the boat and have the bride bolting before she said "I do."

Then Dan took his bride's hands and looked deeply into her eyes. "Flora, I know we had beautiful words from Shakespeare that we'd rehearsed for the ceremony, but I want to speak from my heart because over the last few days, I've come to realize just how deeply I do love you.

"I was scared when I thought you were married, so scared and hurt that you didn't share that part of your life with me that I couldn't see straight. Then today, I went for a long walk, and that's when I realized I couldn't put all the pieces together in my mind, but I did know one thing: it was that, without a doubt, you are the only woman that I want to spend the rest of my life with. I know we'll have our ups and downs, Flora. I know there will be heartache and pain, but I want to go through all that with you by my side because you are the only woman that I love, and I can't imagine spending a minute of my life with anybody else."

Flora's eyes filled with tears again. She looked up at Dan and said, her voice barely above a whisper, "When I met you, I remember how in awe I was with how handsome you were. I never imagined in a million years that you would look at me twice. I've read books all of my life and dreamed that one day, I would meet my Prince Charming. But I had no idea how deeply I could feel for somebody and how much I could love you. Not only are you the kindest, gentlest, sweetest man I've ever known, you are my best friend. I want to be the best person I can because when I'm around you, you bring out the best in me. Thank you for loving me. Thank you for forgiving me."

As she finished, there wasn't a dry eye in the house.

Dan leaned forward, pulled up her veil, and kissed her gently on the lips as the whole room erupted into applause.

"Looks like that's it," said Doris, nodding and closing her prayer book. "I now pronounce you husband and wife. Go have fun."

Mrs. Hemlock looked relieved, finally able to play the exit music as they both made their way up the aisle and into the house for hors d'oeuvres and wine. It appeared that Flora had won her battle with the food, too, as it was all laid out in order by color, except for one odd-looking tray that stood out like a sore thumb, garnished with beets and tomatoes.

~

AN HOUR LATER, the chapel had been turned into a place fit for an evening of celebration. As we left the Labettes' house at twilight, a light snow started to fall. The bride looked enchanting as she glided across the lawn with her bridegroom. Lottie and Lavinia had decorated inside with hundreds of minia-ture white twinkling Christmas lights that now illuminated the building. A stage had been erected at the far end of the room, where Flora's jazz band was setting up. Fortunately for us—and unfortunately for Doris—the bongo players had already been booked.

Soon, soft jazz music filled the space, and the newlyweds danced to the song "The Way You Look Tonight."

After the speeches, all the members of the Rejected Writers' Book Club gathered around a table as the band moved into high gear.

"Well," said Ruby, "that seems to have gone off without a hitch."

Everyone stared at her.

"If that's what you call *going off without a hitch*," said Doris, "I don't know what to say. I haven't jogged up and down like that since I was a teenager."

"I think they make a lovely couple," said Annie thoughtfully.

"So do I," said John as he joined the table. "I'm going. I just wanted to say good-bye."

"Going?" I asked.

"Back home. I'm going back where I belong."

"But you told us there was nothing for you there," remarked Lavinia. "Why would you go back? You should consider staying here."

John smiled. "I think I've caused enough trouble."

"Honey, *trouble* is my middle name," said Lavinia. "And look, they haven't run me out of town yet. Besides," she said, taking his arm and pulling him into the room, "we could do with a good man in our Rejected Writers' Book Club. We don't have anyone who writes detective novels."

"Not even me," said John. "I kind of lied about that, too."

"You don't have to be good to be rejected," she encouraged him. "Just prolific."

"Thank you for the offer," he said, smiling. "But I have some things I need to take care of back home. Being here has helped me see life from a different perspective, and I want to put some things right. Starting with you ladies—my name is actually Darren."

"Well, Darren, you should think about it. You'd be the first man we've ever had," said Lottie smiling.

"You speak for yourself, Lottie," said Lavinia as Lottie blushed and screeched, "Lavinia!" in her high-pitched, rebuking tone. The group dissolved into laughter.

We all gave him a hug and waved to him as he left. Right behind him were Dan's parents, who needed to get back to their bed and breakfast in Medford, along with Marcy, who was pouting and complaining about having a headache.

"All that wedding planning, no doubt," said Annie through gritted teeth as we all waved good-bye to them from the door before rejoining our table.

We sat down to enjoy the rest of the evening. James and

Olivia, my grandchildren's namesakes, who had been bestowed with the honor after helping deliver Stacy's babies, joined us at the table. I couldn't help wondering by the way they were looking at one another if they were maybe secretly seeing each other. James had been a tremendous help in providing us with a theater for our show the year before. He was a lovely man, and I knew they were both single.

Suddenly, Ernie appeared. "So my little whipper snapper." He tapped Doris on the shoulder. "Care to cut a rug with me, for old times' sake?"

Doris waved him away, but before she could protest, he had her by the arm and up on the dance floor. The band broke out into a lively Glen Miller number.

"Fancy joining them?" implored Martin. He absolutely loved Glen Miller. Before I could say no and hold up my casted arm, he grabbed my other hand and pulled me up, too.

The Labette twins jumped up, and we all danced away to "String of Pearls" and filled the little room with the happy sounds of laughter and joy.

Stacy and her children arrived. They had gone back home to change.

"I thought we'd come and join in the fun," she said.

"Wonderful," I said as Grandpa grabbed hold of a twin in each arm and started to dance with them on the dance floor. Chris and Stacy automatically made their way to the dance floor, too, and started to dance together, giggling with each other as they continued to interact with their kids.

Suddenly, a hand was upon my shoulder. I spun around, and both Flora and Dan gave me a hug.

"Flora and I just wanted to thank you for everything you've done for us over the years. Without you, I don't think we could have pulled this off. We're so grateful."

I started to tear up again.

"We are going to sneak out to the hotel while everybody is still having a good time," Flora added.

I followed them to the chapel door as the band took a break. Olivia sat at the grand piano to play soft Christmas music as an interlude. Her first song was an eloquent version of "O Holy Night." The soft strains filled the room as I opened the door for the bride and groom. As they waved their good-byes, I noticed the snow was falling heavier now, and it surrounded them like white fluffy clouds. It clung to Flora's veil and Dan's dark hair as they raced to their little silver-blue car that would take them to their hotel and their wedding night.

As I turned and looked around the room in wonder, tears welled up within me and started to catch in my throat. In all its craziness, and for all the wild adventures that this group and this town had sent me on, I'd loved being part of it all.

Doris was busy dancing and laughing with Ernie. Annie was happy, knitting at the table. Ethel's face registered horror as June Horton described in great detail her latest Google-diagnosed illness. On the dance floor, the Labette twins were now jiving together, and Ruby, twirling in circles, was in her own world, wearing a beautiful white satin outfit that she had re-created from Doris's wedding dress.

I took a last deep breath of the frigid air as I closed the door. Yes, this was the community of Southlea Bay in all its glory, with its loves and its losses, its joy and its sadness, and its ordinary and very extraordinary, and there was definitely no other place on earth I would rather be.

The End

ACKNOWLEDGMENTS

When you read a book, you hear just one voice: the voice of the author. But so many people work tirelessly together to blend and coax out that voice, crafting it into one clear thread that becomes the story that you read. It really is a team effort, and I'm grateful for the team that works with me every day.

First and foremost, I have to thank my husband, Matthew Wilson. He is my number one fan and cosupporter. Thank you for the cleaning you've done, for the dinners that you've cooked, and for your awesome parenting, which has allowed me to burn the midnight oil in order to finish a book on my latest deadline. I can't even imagine what it must be like to not have such a supportive partner and caring husband; I appreciate you every day.

Also to my son, Christopher, who at one point looked at the growing pile of laundry and decided it was time to start doing it himself. Thank you, son, for your editorial eye, your quick wit, your patience as your mother finishes "just one more paragraph." Thank you both for your love, support, and laughter that keeps me writing every day.

To my wonderful agent, Andrea Hurst, and her amazing team

of merry men and women, especially Sean Fletcher and Rebecca Berus, who have continued to support me through this three-book series—from trips down to the Amazon building, where we got caught in game traffic, to all your stellar tips on marketing and publishing.

To my own little editorial team: Cate Perry, for the fabulous job you did on my developmental edits and for writing the words *LOL* so many times in your comments that it kept me going when I hit edit number 563; and also to my line editor, Audrey Mackaman. Thank you for your expertise and the speed with which you turned this around.

Also to my fabulous team at Lake Union Publishing, who have been encouraging me throughout this series' journey. My gratitude goes first to my acquisitions editor and the editorial director at Lake Union, Danielle Marshall, whose enthusiasm and professionalism light up my world; and to my author liaison, Gabe Dumpit, thank you for always being on the other end of an email and for your constant support and encouragement.

To my Lake Union marketing team, who can still get my book to number one even when it's been published for over a year. You guys are awesome. And my thanks also go to Mariëtte Franken and all the editorial team at Kindle Press.

To my best writing buddy, KJ Waters: You are always the first person I reach out to when something in my writing world happens, which proves we must be the best of friends. Thank you for sharing my joys and sharing my losses. I'm glad that we get to walk this author path together.

To my book cover design team at Blondie's Custom Book Covers, KJ Waters, and Jody Smyers, thanks for the laughs and all the amazing work you did making the cover look so incredible. You guys rock.

To all my fellow authors at the Ladies of the Lake, especially Kerry Schafer, Camille di Mio, Carol Mason, Steena Holmes, Marilyn Simon Rothstein and Patricia Sands, thank you for your support and encouragement throughout the year and for keeping me sane and laughing.

To my fabulous friend Melinda Mack, who is always my emotional support and one of my greatest cheerleaders; and also to my dear friend Eric, who not only keeps me laughing through the process, but also has the best advice for everything, from life to my work.

To my mom, Anne Drummond, and my sisters, Gemma and Jo: thank you for all your love and support over the years.

Lastly, to you, my readers: So many times, I've wondered if I'll keep going, and often it's one of your wonderful reviews that will pull me through. My favorites are about how much you are laughing. I hope to keep you laughing for a long time to come.

BOOK CLUB QUESTIONS

1. What were the themes of this book?

2. What did you think of the structure and style of the writing?

3. What scene was the most pivotal for the book?

4. What surprised you the most about the story?

5. Did any of the characters remind you of yourself or someone you know? How?

6. Did you disagree with the choices of any of the characters?

7. What past influences are shaping the actions of the characters in the story?

8. How have the characters changed by the end of the book?

9. Are there any books that you would compare this one to?

10. Have you read any other books by this author? How does this one compare?

11. What did you learn from, take away from, or get out of this book?

12. Would you recommend this book to a friend?

ABOUT THE AUTHOR

Suzanne Kelman is the bestselling author of the Southlea Bay series and an award-winning screenwriter and playwright. Born and raised in the United Kingdom she now lives in Washington State in her own version of Southlea Bay with her husband Matthew; her son Christopher; and a menagerie of rescued animals. She enjoys theatre and high teas, and she can sing the first verse of "Puff, the Magic Dragon" backwards.

facebook.com/suzanne.kelman.5

twitter.com/suzkelman

instagram.com/suzkelman

amazon.com/author/suzannekelman

goodreads.com/SuzanneKelman

Made in the USA
Middletown, DE
12 November 2020